LOST IN
GHOSTVILLE

BY JOHN BLADEK

raintree

a Capstone company   publishers for children

Raintree is an imprint of Capstone Global Library Limited, a company incorporated
in England and Wales having its registered office at 264 Banbury Road, Oxford OX2
7DY – Registered company number: 6695582

www.raintree.co.uk
myorders@raintree.co.uk

ISBN 978-1-4747-2440-1 (paperback)
ISBN 978-1-4747-2441-8 (ebook)

Printed and bound in China.
20 19 18 17 16
10 9 8 7 6 5 4 3 2 1

A CIP catalogue for this book is available from the
British Library.

Designer: Kristi Carlson
Cover Illustrator: Charlie Bowater
Design Element: Shutterstock: Reinhold Leitner

To Mom and Dad, wishing you were here.

CONTENTS

CHAPTER ONE

A GHOST IN THE GIRLS' TOILETS

I looked around the classroom. All the Year 7 pupils sat up straight at their desks and chewed on pens or picked noses, waiting for our weekly maths test. My teacher, Mr Brakenbush, glanced at the clock and leaned over to scoop up a pile of papers. A tiny beep went off in my pocket. I had to go.

I threw up my hand.

"No, Dan." Mr Brakenbush rolled his eyes. "You cannot go to the toilet. We're taking a test."

"But I really have to go . . . right now." I crossed my legs to look like I was holding it in.

Mr Brakenbush grunted. "Quiet, Dan. You should have gone before."

"I forgot."

He drummed his fingers on his desk and stared up at the ceiling. I squirmed and pulled my hair and puffed my cheeks, wondering how best to look like I was about to burst. When the ecto-meter sounded I only had minutes, if not seconds, before the ectoplasmic signal dissipated and I lost my chance. A toilet emergency was always the best way to get out of class.

After half a minute of watching me dance in my chair, Mr Brakenbush sighed and dropped his left eyebrow, the really bushy one. The one with the bird's nest in it.

My pocket beeped again. Hunching over to cover the sound, I checked Brakenbush's eyebrow for any sign that he'd heard.

"I'll go with him," Luke said. "Make sure he doesn't dawdle." Luke's been my best friend since I wandered into his back garden when we were three. He'll take any excuse to get away from a test, even using words like "dawdle".

"Be quiet and keep your eyes on your own test, Luke." Mr Brakenbush nodded at me. "Go, Mr Newton. You have three minutes before your grade drops."

I checked the clock and made for the door. Luke snagged my sleeve on the way by. "Get me some chocolate from the machine."

"There's no chocolate in the machine, just nutritious stuff."

"Two minutes, forty-five seconds." Mr Brakenbush tapped his watch. "Don't make me change my mind."

"Gotta go." I shot out of the room like water from a fire hose.

Once I'd cleared Mr Brakenbush's wee-stopping gaze, I pulled out my ecto-meter and checked the readings. It was beeping like mad and the screen on my mobile ghost tracker showed a bouncy green line and a series of six numbers. I had no idea what the numbers were for, probably an error code, but the line peak meant a ghost was nearby.

I have this goal to scientifically prove that ghosts are real. I'd found some really great ghost-finders that the pros use online: the Ghost-O-Cator and the Spector-Detector. But since Dad lost his job he's talked a lot about making sacrifices, and I suppose £300 for a super detector was my sacrifice. So I looked up the plans on the Internet and built my own. The only thing I didn't have was an infrared camera to photograph the ghost. But I had my mobile phone camera, so no problem.

I peeked around the corner. The corridor was clear. The signal had to be coming from behind the next door.

I reached out and grabbed . . .

I froze solid. Staring me down was a great big humongous *GIRLS* sign. Nothing stops a boy faster than the most secret place on earth – the girls' toilets. I checked the signal again. Strong and clear, the biggest I'd ever seen. This was the best chance I'd ever had of finding a ghost. I inched closer. Why did it have to be in the girls' toilets?

I imagined the doom that would drop from the sky if I got caught in the *Mysterious Chamber*. The rack, thumb screws – anything was possible. I could just say that I was lost, you know, blinded by my need to wee. But Luke and I had pretty much used every excuse in the book from all the times we'd "accidentally" got into trouble, and I don't think Mr Brakenbush was listening anymore. And, let's face it, teachers kind of expect you to know which toilet is which by Year 7. On the other hand, it wasn't break time, so maybe no one was in there. I mean, what teacher lets pupils out during class?

My mobile phone buzzed. I checked the screen but all it said was, *No name.*

"Hello?"

"One and a half minutes left, Mr Newton. I hope everything is coming out okay."

I thought we weren't supposed to use phones at school. Didn't Mr Brakenbush know the rules?

"Almost done." I needed more time. "I think they're out of paper towels. Should I go and get some?"

"You're wearing trousers, use them."

Click. He hung up.

Beep, beep, beeeeeeeep!

The signal was blasting and I was running out of time.

The sign still said *GIRLS*.

According to my favourite TV show host, Rex Rangler, who's totally cool on the science programmes *Spirit Trackers* and *Dinosaur Diggin'*, chances like this may come along only once. Rex has found lots of ghosts, but never got any video of them because they go into hiding when the cameras turn on. All that equipment scares them away. That's why I made my ecto-meter extra small and easy to hide. It pretty much looked like a mobile phone – my dad's ancient mobile phone – no touch screen. I planned to find a real ghost, then show Rex

Rangler himself when my class visited the grand opening of his new Dino Barn right here in town. I could be rich and famous, and then Dad wouldn't have to worry about being out of work anymore. But this might be my only chance.

Ghosts, or GIRLS?

Beep, beep.

Uh-oh. The signal shrank like a leaky balloon.

The ghost was fading away. I had to risk it. I crossed my fingers and hoped that the room was clear of the living.

I took a deep breath, then whipped out my mobile phone camera and kicked open the door.

"Get out of here, you freak!" Vicki Winters, all spit and flying hair, splashed a handful of water from the sink at me. "I'm telling!"

Rats. No ghosts, just *GIRLS*.

Unless Vicki Winters was a ghost! I'd thought that she was just a really, really annoying girl. But if she was a ghost that would explain why she'd done so well on tests. When you repeat Year 7 for a century, you pick up a lot of answers.

Vicki screamed again and hit me with a wet paper towel. "Idiot! You're going to get it!"

In a flash two more girls appeared, Jessica and Allison, both shrieking. "Fig Newton! You creep!" Jessica's always screaming.

Did Mr Brakenbush let everyone out of class?

"Get lost!" Vicki took a swipe at my phone. Then all three girls ran down the corridor like their hair was on fire.

Beep beep.

The ecto-meter still showed something here. I clicked a couple of quick pictures and headed back to class. Maybe I could still be famous.

CHAPTER TWO

NO PICTURES!

After my ghost expedition to the girls' toilets I still managed to get a B on my test. It turned out I really did have to go to the toilet, so I was a bit late. And, of course, Vicki told the teacher about me.

Apparently taking pictures in the girls' toilets gets you detention *and* your phone and ecto-meter taken away, even if you waited to click the pics until everyone had left. How was I supposed to track down the school's spirits without my equipment? And worse, I couldn't show Rex Rangler my valuable data! How was I going to get on TV? The injustice just piled higher and higher.

"Mate," Luke said during afternoon break while we played football on the playground. "That was so amazing. The girls' toilets. I can't believe it. That's the coolest. Wish I could have gone."

Too bad Mr Brakenbush wasn't as much fun as Luke.

"I had to lick envelopes in the head teacher's office for

the *Save our Historic Buildings* fundraiser," I said. There is definitely no "fun" in "fundraiser". "And now I can't go on the field trip to the Dino Barn sneak peek."

"That's so annoying. It's totally Vicki's fault. Why is she such a nerd?"

"I don't know," I said. "It's not like I saw anything. She was only washing her hands."

"Who am I going to hang out with now?" Luke asked.

His concern for me was overwhelming. I got to spend time with the head teacher.

The Dino Barn was supposed to be the coolest place ever conceived. Not only did the ads say it had *real* dinosaur skeletons and teeth and horns and even petrified poo, but it also had those robot dinosaurs that really moved and ate each other. It sounded totally cool and scientific, but most importantly, Rex Rangler owned it. Our whole class was going on Friday, in two days.

"It's not fair. It's not like I'm the only boy who ever wandered into the girls' toilets," I said.

"The only one with a camera," Luke said.

"I waited until the girls left before I took any pictures."

"That was dumb." Luke said with a loud snort. "Too

bad your mum's not driving. Then they'd have to let you go."

I was nearly blinded by the brilliance of the light bulb going off. I slapped Luke on the back. "That's it! Great thinking. I will be going to the Dino Barn *and* talking to Rex Rangler."

★ ★ ★

"All right, class," Mr Brakenbush said early Friday morning. "Quiet down and line up. Volunteer parents are here to take us to the Dinosaur Barn. Let's show them how well behaved pupils at Richard Adams Secondary School can be."

Everyone chanted. "Dino Barn, Dino Barn. It's not the farm, it's Dino Barn!"

"Thank you for reminding me that you watch too much TV," Mr Brakenbush said.

I smiled and lined up. My plan had worked. Mum had some time to drive in between showing houses for her estate agent's job. It wasn't perfect. I'd had to do double duty stamp licking and my tongue was still sticking to my lips. I also didn't have my ecto-meter and Luke was going in a different car. And Vicki, little Miss Perfect-who-gets-people-into-trouble-after-they-innocently-wandered-into-the-girls'-room-on-a-scientific-quest, was travelling with me. But at least I was going.

Luke was excited too. He reached into his pocket and pulled out a lump of something yellowishly grey-green, sort of like vomit, but more solid and without chunks. "Know what this is?"

"Your lunch?"

Luke took a sniff. "Good guess. But I like mayonnaise with my peanut butter. Try again." He waved the gunk in my face. I shrugged.

"It's real live fake dino poo." He grinned so much I thought he *was* going to eat it. "I ordered it online."

"Really? Too bad it only looks like dino poo. Didn't they have any that smelled, too?"

Luke's smile drooped. "No, I checked."

I glanced over at Vicki. She was waving her arm at Mr Brakenbush. She can't resist raising her hand. She probably wanted to tell him all about dinosaur mummies or something else she'd already bored us with in class. Some people read too much.

Grinning, Luke handed me a clump of his dino poo. "Here. You can get back at Vicki."

I tried to push it away. "I'm in trouble already." Luke pushed harder so I finally grabbed the poo.

Just then I heard a car horn. Mum's car whipped into the car park and screeched to a stop. I shoved the goo into my pocket before Mr Brakenbush saw.

"Hi, Honeybunch," Mum said, right in front of everyone. Didn't she know people were listening? It was bad enough Jessica called me Fig Newton. I didn't want to give her any more ammunition. I ducked into the front seat before Mum could say anything else embarrassing.

Mr Brakenbush knocked on the window. "Here's one more passenger, Mrs Newton." Vicki frowned and slipped into the back seat as Mr Brakenbush handed my mum a piece of paper. "These are the directions to the Dino Barn."

"I got the text," Mum said, cutting him off. "You keep those for someone who needs them." Then she rolled up the window and we shot into the street.

I leaned back and thought about how I'd get Rex

Rangler to come and look for ghosts with me. Without my ecto-meter data it would be a tough sell. I'd have to convince him that the ghosts in the girls' toilets were real. I glanced at Vicki. Too bad she wasn't a ghost.

I was glad I was sitting in the front. Vicki sat in the back and gave her know-it-all guided tour of our route.

"And that's the old Crenshaw mansion." She pointed at an ancient house surrounded by an iron fence. It looked like a prison, but with nice shrubs. "Blanding Crenshaw was a railway tycoon who built his mansion in 1887, made entirely out of railway sleepers and . . ."

Mum zoomed by. She liked to drive fast, which was cool. And it cut off Vicki before she could finish, which was cooler.

I ignored Vicki and imagined my conversation with Rex Rangler as best I could, but she kept talking. "They're tearing down all these old buildings from the 1890s to build a new shopping centre. See, some of the houses are already gone. That's why I helped to organize the *Save our Historic Buildings* fundraiser at school. We're trying to get them to build the shopping centre somewhere else."

Vicki was behind the envelope licking? She got me into trouble, and then made up my punishment? I took a quick look at the dino poo Luke gave me. Maybe . . .

Then Mum had to go and encourage her. "But we need that shopping centre. It's being built by that man who runs the Dino Barn, Rex Rangler. It's a great idea."

Wow, Rex Rangler was doing everything. He was cooler than I thought.

"But he's destroying our town's history," Vicki said. "Look, there's the old library."

I looked out at an old brick building, half knocked down by a wrecking ball. I wished I could have seen it getting smashed. That would have been cool.

"He's just a TV presenter," Vicki said. "He doesn't know anything about urban development or conservation, or even dinosaurs probably. He just reads scripts that cleverer people write."

She pointed out of the window at more crumbling buildings. They pretty much looked like they were going to fall down on their own. Why not give them some help? And Rex was not *just* a TV presenter. He knew everything about dinosaurs, and *ghosts*.

"Those buildings are all architecturally significant," Vicki said. "Without them we'll be just like every other shopping-centre-plagued city in the country."

"Those cities have jobs, dear," Mum said. "We can't afford to pass any up."

I knew she was talking about Dad. The bottling plant laid him off almost six months ago and he worried about money all the time. He couldn't drive today because he was looking for a job. He was always looking for a job.

Mum went into lecture mode. "You're too young to understand how important this project is for this town. Mr Rangler is using his fame to rebuild the city. Why, he even tore down my mother's old house and paid us good money."

I looked out the window. My grandma's house was the one old building I did care about. I used to visit all the time and she'd bake cookies and read me stories in front of the fireplace. Tales of heroes saving the world and funny stories of children who always messed up.

I liked the ghost stories the best. Grandma always made spooky noises and let me wear old sheets and we'd play hide-and-seek. That's when I first decided to look for ghosts. But Grandma wasn't there anymore. She wasn't anywhere.

After a couple of minutes the car jerked to a halt and Mum said, "Here we are."

Out of my window I saw a row of shrubs and a chain-link fence. "Are you sure?"

"There's nothing here," Vicki said.

"This is the place." Mum shooed me out of the door. "The school texted the address: 21 Antique Ave. It's just around the corner and through the gate. I've got to hurry. I'll pick you two up at one o'clock sharp. Don't be late." She leaned out of the window and blew me a kiss. "Things to do, clients to see. You can give me a report when I come back. Bye Honeybunch."

She sped off, leaving me and Vicki standing on the pavement with the name Honeybunch hanging in the air like a nerd balloon.

"I don't see any other children," Vicki said.

"We're just early." I really wished Luke would get here soon.

We walked halfway down the street to the end of the fence and through the gate. Vicki stopped and gasped, staring wide-eyed at an old two-storey building with peeling paint squatting in the middle of an empty car park. The awning over the entrance sagged and weeds were growing everywhere. "Oh no. This is the wrong place," she said.

The car park was completely deserted and I didn't see any lights. Then I spotted a faded sign over the entrance.

"Look, it says *Museum*. And this is 21 Antique Ave. This has to be it." I pulled out my ticket.

"Do you see anyone?" she asked.

"They'll show up. We can wait inside."

Vicki crossed her arms and kicked at the ground, frowning. "Mr Brakenbush better get here. And if you touch me with Luke's goop, I'll break your arm, Honeybunch."

CHAPTER THREE

THIS WAY TO
THE EGRESS

Vicki and I walked up to the museum and looked around, waiting for the rest of my class to show up. I peered through the glass of the ticket window. Everything was dark and covered with dust, a great place for a ghost. Rex Rangler probably set it up that way. He's a genius.

"This is awful," Vicki said. "What are we doing here? This isn't the Dino Barn."

I brushed the cobwebs off the front door and spotted a light and some movement. "The sign says *Museum*. And the Dino Barn is a sort of museum. I think I see someone. Besides, this place is old, just like all those other old buildings you've got people licking envelopes for."

Vicki crossed her arms and glared at me. "Just because I want to save historic buildings doesn't mean we're not lost."

Her logic escaped me. "I'm going inside to talk to Rex Rangler about ghosts." I pushed open the door and walked in.

The inside of the Dino Barn looked as deserted as the outside. Vicki dragged her feet but followed me into a big lobby bathed in the light of a sign flashing neon red.

WELCOME: THIS WAY TO THE EGRESS

"Egress? Cool," I said. "See, this is the right place. I bet that's one of the new dinosaur robot exhibits. I hope it's something with big teeth and claws."

"Egress means exit." Vicki had a grammar-teacher fun-ruining voice.

"That doesn't make any sense. You sure it's not another word for 'robot'?"

"They want you to leave as soon as you come so you have to pay to get back in again," she said. "It's an old trick. P.T. Barnum used it in his museum in the 1840s."

"You were there?"

"I *read* about it."

That egress story sounded like a pile of unlicked envelopes. I clutched my ticket.

"May I help you?" a voice said behind me.

I nearly wet my pants. Vicki hit the ceiling. Spinning around I saw a tall man with white hair and white eyes and white . . . everything, except his black suit, which looked older and dustier than the building. He stared at me while holding out his hand.

"Oh, you must be the ticket taker," I said after I started breathing again.

I handed him my ticket. "I've already paid. We're from Year 7 at Richard Adams Secondary School on a field trip and I'd like to talk to Rex Rangler."

The man kept his hand out but didn't take my ticket, so I flipped it at him. It fell straight to the floor.

"Oops, I'll get it." I picked up the ticket, then reached out to drop it in his hand.

The man just stared at me. I'd never seen anyone so pale, or dusty. His hair had cobwebs.

"Are you here for the matinee?" He was so thin, his mouth was wider than his head and his teeth stuck out beyond his cheeks when he talked. "You're early. The film doesn't start for another hour." He glared down at me like he knew I always sneaked sweets into the cinema.

I glanced at Vicki. She was as pale as the ticket taker. I suppose he really scared her. I'd have to tell Luke, but would skip the part where I almost wet my pants.

"There's a film?" I asked. "Cool. We'll just have a look at the dinosaurs until then."

"Refreshments are available to your left." He pointed off towards an empty counter. Then he turned and walked off into the dark.

That was creepy. That bloke looked as old as the dinosaurs. I wondered where they were.

Vicki stood still and stared in the direction the ticket taker had vanished. "I think I've seen him before. He used to own the old cinema, the one they're tearing down. My mum and dad took me to see old films there before . . .." She stopped and looked away.

"Wow, that sounds like fun," I said, rolling my eyes. Actually it did. We hadn't gone to the cinema since Dad lost his job. It cost too much. Grandma used to come with us and sit next to me. Sometimes, when I was little, she'd hold my hand during the scary parts. She said I made her feel brave, but I felt better, too.

"Old films? Did they sell old popcorn, too?"

Vicki glared at me. "Stuff doesn't have to be new to be fun."

I had to disagree.

"If he owned a cinema, you'd think he'd be better at taking tickets." I noticed that Vicki still held hers.

"Maybe," Vicki said. "But there was something else about him I can't remember."

"Really? That's a first. Wasn't he old enough?"

Vicki curled her lip. "Why are you against old things?"

"I'm not, not all old things anyway. I like ghosts, and they're old. But I can't look for them because you got my ecto-meter taken away."

"Is that what you were using to spy on me in the girls' toilets?" she asked. "An ecto-meter?"

"No! It's for finding ghosts. And I wasn't spying."

"Could've fooled me," she said. "Is that why everyone thinks you're an idiot?"

"Not as big an idiot as you."

Vicki's eyes flared and she punched me in the shoulder, about twice as hard as Luke ever had. I tried not to squeal, but I think I let out a little "eek" anyway. Vicki took off in the same direction as the ticket taker, leaving me behind. She screamed over her shoulder, "I am not an idiot! And it's too bad you don't have your ecto-meter. Because you just saw a ghost."

I froze and stopped rubbing my wound.

Ghost?

But Vicki was gone. She'd disappeared into the dark.

CHAPTER FOUR

GHOST?

Vicki ran off just because I'd called her an idiot. If Luke and I ran away every time we called each other a name, we'd have never met.

And what did she mean I'd seen a ghost? That ticket taker was weird and rubbish at his job – I noticed my ticket lying on the ground – but he wasn't a ghost. Ghosts aren't people anymore. According to *Spirit Trackers*, they're an ecto-magnetic paranormal phenomena that mimic the people they used to be, sort of a person echo. Vicki didn't know what she was talking about. If she wanted to run off, she'd have to find her own way back.

I still didn't see anyone else. Where was Mr Brakenbush? I thought this was the right place now that someone had taken my ticket. But where was my class?

"'Scuse me, son," a voice said from down the dark corridor. "I can see you're busy contemplating terrifically important things, but do you think you could give a tired old railway man a hand?"

I peered down the black passage. It looked empty. "Who's there?"

A bearded man wearing a battered old jacket and a hat appeared out of the blackness. He stuck his hand out for me to shake. "Name's Richard Adams."

"That's weird. My school's got that same name."

"Really? Imagine that." His eyes twinkled.

"What kind of help did you need?"

"Much obliged," he said, smiling. "You're a kind fellow and I'm in your debt. Been waiting for you to come and help me out." He slipped off his hat and wiped his forehead with his arm. I couldn't tell which was greasier. "Wasn't sure you'd make it."

"Um, yeah." I glanced over his shoulder, looking for Vicki.

"Your friend went that way." He pointed down the corridor. "Seemed to be in a hurry."

"She's not really my friend."

He grinned at me, scratching his beard. "I was wondering if you could help me get out of this place."

"Don't you work here at the Dino Barn?" I thought employees should know about the egress.

"Work here? Oh no, no, no. Haven't worked in years. Sort of a freelancer you might say. And this isn't any Dino Barn, whatever that is."

"It's not?" Oh no. Vicki was right. We really were in the wrong place. "What is it?"

The man pulled out a pipe and tapped it against his palm. "Don't honestly know. I'm a bit lost myself."

"Oh, well the egress is back that way."

"The egress, eh," he said with a grin. "Aren't you a fancy talker? Must be a good school that has my name."

Vicki might be on to something. Talking with big words made me feel clever. But maybe that was her problem. Her words made her feel clever even when she wasn't.

"Point the way and I'll follow." He bowed and waited.

"She hasn't come back yet," I said. "I kind of need her so we can get to the Dino Barn."

"Don't worry. Can't get lost in here."

Can't get lost? Then why did he just say he was lost? This bloke was starting to creep me out. Everyone here was weird. I walked back towards the big neon sign and pointed to the doors. "That's the way out."

Adams scratched his chin and stared at the doors, not moving. I turned to go back and look for Vicki. "Bye."

"I wonder if you could do an old man one more small favour?" He tilted his head with one eye shut as he squinted at the door. "These old hands just don't work like they used to. Might you open the door for me?"

"Of course." I felt like I was in scouts again. I hadn't gone since Luke and I had accidentally burned down our tent with a flaming marshmallow bomb last summer. Maybe this was worth a merit badge.

As the man reached the door, his eyes went wide and a screeching, sucking sound blasted my ears. He grabbed at me, but before he could take my hand, his whole body stretched out thinly, like wet spaghetti, and began to swirl. He cried out as he was pulled like toffee, vacuumed back inside the building. In a second he was gone.

I stood there in the doorway, staring back inside. My heart pounded like ten thousand drums.

Vicki walked up behind me. She was already outside. I jumped in the air when she grabbed the door.

"You don't have to hold the door. I'm not going back in."

"It's not for you. It's for . . ."

"What's wrong? You look like you saw another ghost," Vicki said, her eyes wide.

"I think I did."

CHAPTER FIVE

GHOST HUNT

I knew I didn't have any real scientific proof that Adams was a ghost, and ectoplasm wasn't supposed to talk, but the whole spaghetti thing was weird enough to make me wonder. You don't see someone stretched into a noodle every day. I took a deep breath and shook off the clenching in my stomach, telling myself that ghosts were just an ectoplasmic recording and nothing to be scared of. After I calmed down, I realized that going to the wrong place was turning out better than I thought. If there was a real ghost, maybe I could still get on TV.

"What did you see?" Vicki asked.

"I saw a weird-looking old bloke get sucked up like spaghetti. Then he just vanished into thin air."

"Wow. Then there are two ghosts."

"Just one," I said. "The ticket taker isn't a ghost."

"How do you know yours was a ghost and the ticket taker wasn't?" Vicki asked with a frown. "I think you just don't want to admit that I found a ghost first."

"You wouldn't understand. Ghosts are complicated."

"So?"

"So I'm an expert, and you're not."

Vicki glared at me and tried to blow a bubble with her gum. She pursed her lips and puffed her cheeks, firing a big wad of spit-covered pink out of her mouth. The blob hit me right between the eyes.

"Sorry. I'm not very good at bubbles."

"No, really?" I said, wiping off her spit. I thought again about the dino poo in my pocket.

Vicki unwrapped another piece of gum and popped it into her mouth. "If you're the expert, have you ever seen a ghost before?" She smacked her new piece of gum.

"No." I admitted that too fast. "I mean, not in person anyway. But I know all about them. My grandma taught me that spooky ghost stories are just for fun. Real ghosts are a natural phenomenon, leftover signals trapped in rocks and stuff."

"Rocks?" Vicki asked, her face screwed up like she didn't believe me.

"Yep. In the ground. The signals, ectoplasm and things, leak out and that's a ghost."

"Um," Vicki said. "Then I suppose it's too bad you got your ecto-meter taken away; we could have used it."

I scowled. "You mean too bad *you* got it taken away."

"You were the one taking pictures in the girls' toilets. And I didn't tell Mr Brakenbush. It was Jessica."

Jessica? I should have known it was her. She'd been telling on me and Luke since Year 2 and the "jam and spider" incident. Luke had put jam on a dozen spiders we'd captured outside and put them in Jessica's pencil holder. She screamed for a month. Luke had got me into a lot of trouble, but he didn't spit on me – very much. But if Vicki didn't tell on me and she really was interested in ghosts, maybe she wasn't all bad.

"I still don't have my ecto-meter," I said.

"That's okay," Vicki said. "Those ghost detectors don't work eighty-seven per cent of the time, and the other thirteen per cent they're wrong."

What? Eighty-seven and thirteen was almost . . .

"That's not true. This is science. I've seen it on TV. How do you know anyway?"

"Just 'cause." Vicki shifted her eyes back and forth. "Do you think ghosts would hurt people?"

"No," I said. "They can't. They aren't solid, just ectoplasm."

"You keep saying 'ectoplasm'," Vicki said. "Do you even know what it is?"

"Of course," I told her. "It's ghost stuff."

Vicki rolled her eyes. Like she knew better than *Spirit Trackers*. She bit her lip. "Umm, do you think people come back as ghosts, you know, like to visit the people they left behind?"

I shook my head. "No, I told you. Ghosts are paranormal phenomena, not people anymore. They might look like people, but they're really just a sort of leftover reflection."

"Are you sure?"

"Yeah. Rex Rangler said so on TV. Now I want to find that ghost. You can wait here if you like."

I started to walk away when Vicki rushed up and grabbed my arm. "That's okay. I'll help. I don't want to wait alone."

"Scared?" Her fingers were leaving claw marks.

"No. Are you?" she asked.

"Nope." This was what I'd always wanted.

"Good, then let's look for ghosts," she said.

I pried my arm out of Vicki's vice-like grip and looked around, but I wasn't sure what I was searching for. The main lobby was lit by the neon sign, but down the corridor everything was dark. Then I saw it. A series of impressions in the dust trailed around in a circle in the middle of the floor.

"Look, footprints. The ticket taker can't be a ghost if he left footprints."

Vicki walked over and put her foot into one of the prints. "These are our prints. And there are only two sets. And it proves that the ticket taker is a ghost, unless he can fly."

I put my foot in a print. I'd have noticed that if it hadn't been so dark.

"It also proves that we're in the wrong place," Vicki said. "If this was the Dino Barn they'd dust the floors once in a while."

Not only was Vicki a know-it-all, but a clean-freak know-it-all.

"I already knew that."

"What?"

"The ghost told me this wasn't the Dino Barn," I said. "See? You don't know everything."

"If ghosts are just reflections leaking out of rocks, then how did one talk to you?" she asked.

"They're sound recordings too," I said. "Everyone knows that." I turned and walked down the corridor while Vicki sneered. Did she have to question everything I said?

Empty glass cases lined the walls. I wondered what kind of museum this had been. There were no exhibits left, just the display covers. I passed a hundred-year-old hot dog sitting under a broken heat lamp. Maybe it was a fast-food museum. "Hey, look. It's the ghost of a sausage."

Vicki giggled. "It sort of looks like the ticket taker, only not as skinny."

"Ha. Good one." She was sort of funny, and not just funny looking. "And with a much smaller nose."

We both laughed. Leaving the haunted hot dog, I peeked into a couple of doors. All I found was a broom cupboard and another girls' toilet. "Don't tell on me," I said. "I'm going in." I pushed open the door. It was too dark to see and after a couple of steps I banged into the sink. Something skittered up my arm and over my shoulder. "What was that?" I ran back out into the corridor, shaking my arm and brushing wildly at my back. "Get it off!"

Vicki cringed. "Hold still."

"Get it off!"

She hesitated, then finally let out a shriek and as her eyes closed she swiped at my shoulder. "Oh, gross!" she said. A spider the size of my fist jumped off and raced past my feet. Ghosts might not be scary, but spiders are killers.

"Thanks," I said, imagining being eaten alive by an eight-legged hairball. "You're right. I shouldn't be going into the girls' toilets anymore."

Vicki smiled. "I didn't really mind the toilets thing. It was kind of funny."

"I didn't get in that much trouble," I said. "And I got to see inside the girls' toilets and live."

"It's just a toilet," she said. "I don't think they're so cool."

"That's because you're a girl."

Vicki rolled her eyes again and glanced at an old clock without any hands. "Maybe we should go and find the real Dino Barn. Mr Brakenbush is probably wondering where we are. We could come back later and look for ghosts."

I didn't want to pass up another chance at a ghost. "Let's look for five more minutes. Then we can leave."

"Okay." Vicki sighed. "What were we doing before? We must have done something to bring that ghost out."

I tried to think. "Nothing, just standing around looking lost. I had my ticket . . ."

"May I help you?" a familiar voice said from behind me. Spinning around I saw that same pale man in the dusty black suit, thin as a pencil with a beak nose. He was still waiting for our tickets.

Although I knew he was just a kind of recording, I was still creeped out.

Vicki stared wide-eyed at him for a moment, then raised her hand. We weren't even in school and she still raised her hand. "Are you Mr Greensocks, the owner of the Bijou Cinema?"

He arched his eyebrows and pursed his lips at her, like

Mr Brakenbush does after six hours of hand-raising.

She cringed and took a step back.

"Of course I am, child. The matinee is in an hour. No chewing gum in the cinema."

I snorted. Vicki finally got into trouble for something. Then he looked back at me. "Come this way. We've been waiting." He turned and walked towards a dark stairway at the end of the hall.

"Who's been waiting?" Vicki called after him. He didn't answer.

Vicki grabbed my arm. "Now I remember. Mr Greensocks was that cinema owner. He always made me spit out my gum. He died last year."

I glanced down at the floor. No prints.

CHAPTER SIX

RICHARD ADAMS

Vicki and I walked up the steps of the museum, following the ghost of the ticket taker. Dust from the floor as thick as on the pale man drifted up my nose.

"Achooooo!" I sneezed right on Vicki's shoulder.

"You are so grooooosssss!"

"At least I didn't spit gum on you."

Vicki grinned and stuck her tongue out at me. "Now we're even."

"Come this way." The man's voice echoed out of the dark like he was talking through a rolled-up newspaper. I still couldn't see him. "Time is short."

The first floor was much creepier than the ground floor. The only light came from papered-over windows, and spiderwebs hung from everything. I slapped at my ears and brushed my hair as I imagined giant tarantulas laying eggs in my brain. Vicki shivered and muttered, "Disgusting," every few metres.

We inched our way down the hall until we reached a

door hanging on one hinge. I looked back at Vicki. "You think he's in there?"

"It's too dark to see. You go first," she said.

I put one foot through the opening and stepped into nothing. The door was for a lift shaft!

"AAAAHHHHHHH!"

I threw my arms out and grabbed for the door. I missed but somehow I stopped falling anyway. I felt a tug around my waist. Vicki was holding my belt. With a huge grunt she pulled me back from the abyss.

"You almost killed me!" I said.

"What? I saved you!"

"Only *after* you told me to go first."

"Whatever," Vicki said. "I still saved you. That's twice. You owe me."

"You're wasting time." The ticket taker motioned from another door down the corridor. "We must hurry. You're needed."

I looked at Vicki. "Needed for what?"

She shook her head. "You go first."

"Ha ha. Let's go at the same time." Vicki nodded and we walked down the dark corridor.

This time I checked the floor with my toe before I slipped through the door. Inside sat the man in the old jacket and hat – Richard Adams. He didn't look like spaghetti now. He squatted on the floor, clenching a pipe between his teeth. Although he was mostly a pale white, his teeth were still yellow with brown stains. I'd never heard that ghosts needed to brush and floss. He stirred a small campfire. The fire was floating half a metre off the ground, and I could see through it to the other side. I wished I had my camera. This was the best ghost sighting ever.

"Hello," he said. "I see you found your friend?"

"Uh, she's not really my . . ." I stopped and eyed Vicki. She started to frown. "What happened to you? You looked like you got sucked into a vacuum cleaner."

"A what?"

"You know, a vacuum cleaner. They suck up dirt."

Adams scratched his head. "I don't usually think of myself as dirt. Still, no harm." He held up his arms and spun in a circle to show he was still all there. "But it appears I'm trapped."

"Who are you?" Vicki asked.

"Richard Adams, at your service." He took a slow bow and flourished his hat.

Vicki gasped. "But that's the name of our town's famous railway pioneer. And our school. Richard Adams died one hundred and sixty-five years ago when he fell off his horse after his horse fell off a train."

"That's right." Adams slapped his knee and chuckled. "Someone remembers. I miss that horse, but ol' Samson always was jealous of the railways." He grinned at Vicki, then pulled his pipe out of his mouth and pointed it at her. "I like you."

"Are you two really ghosts?" I asked. Without my ecto-meter I still couldn't be sure. I needed scientific proof.

"Well, of course we are," Adams said. "Proudly dead these many years. There are lots of us dead folk everywhere. Most of the old buildings in town had at least one ghost."

I couldn't believe it. Ghosts everywhere! If it was true, I was going to be famous. But I needed more to get on TV, something I could take and show Rex Rangler. Real scientific evidence.

"Prove it," I said.

Adams lifted off the floor and whooshed by my head. "Isn't this enough to believe?"

"That's pretty good," I said. "But Rex Rangler doesn't let just anybody on TV. I need a video or something to show him. My ecto-meter would have told me if you're a looping visual and sound recording generated by a geo-electromagnetic fingerprint."

Adams squinted at me. "A what? Is that like a vacuum?"

"No," Vicki said, crinkling her nose at me. "He means ectoplasmic rocks."

"Is that what you think I am?" Adams asked.

"Sort of," I said, glaring at Vicki. "That's what real ghosts are."

He paused and looked hard at me, his eyes sad. "You're a tough one to convince. So you don't believe I'm the actual spirit of a man?"

I shook my head. "Nope."

Adams sighed. "You were our last hope."

"What do mean?" I asked.

"We're being hunted."

A cold chill ran through my stomach. "Hunted?"

"That's right," he said with a nod.

"I don't get it. Who's hunting you?" I asked. "Besides us, I mean?"

Adams floated up over my head like a balloon, his arms outstretched in superhero-flying mode. Vicki dodged as he zoomed by. He passed right through her left shoulder. I could see her shudder. After one more spin right through the middle of Mr Greensocks, who gritted his teeth and shook his head, Adams finally stopped his aerial stunts and sat down by his floating fire. He emptied his pipe into mid-air. See-through ashes drifted around the flames, then vanished like they'd never existed.

"I don't know," he said finally. "But they scoured all the haunted places in town and gathered up the ghosts. Men broke into our haunted houses, fancy gizmos *beep-beeping*, and before we even knew what was happening or could warn each other – BAM!" He clapped his hands so hard thunder roared in my ears and Vicki's hair blew back. "All I remember was being pulled and stretched. Next thing I knew I was here, trapped like a rat."

This was getting too cool. "Is that what happened to you at the egress?" Maybe if I could show Rex Rangler the exit that would be enough to get me on TV.

Adams nodded and kicked at his fire, stirring the coals. I saw the flame's reflection in his pale eyes, but the light from it didn't cast a shadow. "Same thing every time I try to leave. Not like the old days at the graveyard. I could come and go as I pleased. Very frustrating."

I'd never checked the cemetery because ghosts weren't supposed to haunt them. Their ectoplasmic remnants hung around where they died, not where they were buried. I'd have to tell Rex Rangler about my new discovery. I was learning so much science.

I also never went to the cemetery because Grandma was there, and I didn't want to see that.

"You haunted a graveyard?" I asked.

"Yep!" Adams said. "That one with my statue at the entrance."

I stared at him.

"The statue that never gets the pigeon poo cleaned off . . . you know, surrounded by the lawn that never gets mowed under the leaves that never get raked."

I shrugged. He sounded like my dad complaining about my gardening.

"I know that cemetery," Vicki said.

"You hang around cemeteries?" I asked her.

"I've been there to pick flowers. And to a different one to visit my . . ." She stopped and looked at her feet. "Never mind. Anyway, cemeteries are important and they're going to pave over that one. I'm sending around a petition." Of course she was.

"Pave over?" Adams shook his head. "Nothing's the same anymore. In my day we had respect for the dead. 'Course in my day I was alive, too, so I didn't really notice."

"Why would anyone kidnap ghosts?" Vicki asked. "I don't get it."

"Neither do I, miss," Adams said. "It's a mystery to me, too."

Missing ghosts sounded like a great TV episode. I looked around the room. "Makes sense to me. Then you wouldn't have to go looking for them. You'd have your own ghosts all the time. So, where are all the other ghosts?"

Adams frowned and patted Mr Greensocks on the shoulder. A cloud of ghost dust flew up and orbited his head. "Just the two of us left. Took the others somewhere, but we hid and they didn't find us. That's what we need you for — to locate our friends and help set us free so we can go back to haunting, or move on."

"Me? Why me?" I asked.

"I heard that you know all about ghosts."

I frowned. Talking ectoplasm was one thing, but . . . "How do you know that?"

"A friend told me," Adams said.

"What friend?"

"Don't you know?" He squinted at me like it was obvious. "She said you used to sit on her lap by the fire and read ghost stories."

My eyes went blurry. I could hardly breathe.

"Grandma?" My voice cracked. "You talked to my grandma? But . . . but she's dead."

"That's right, son. And she needs your help. We all do."

CHAPTER SEVEN

DINO BARN

I stood staring at the two ghosts, shivering at what Adams had just told me about Grandma. Ghost-napped? My stomach lurched like I might be sick. I swallowed hard to keep it in.

I didn't know if I could believe Adams. His story went against everything I'd learned about ghosts. But how could I deny the things that I'd seen? He talked and moved and acted like a real person, except for the floating and passing through solid objects. And how could he know about me and Grandma unless he'd talked to her? And if he'd talked to her, then ghosts really were still people, not just ectoplasm. *Spirit Trackers* was wrong.

I heard a car horn tooting outside. The sound of, "Dan, where are you?" floated through the door.

"We have to go," I said to Vicki. "My mum's here."

"You will help us free my friends, won't you?" Adams took off his hat and wrung it between his hands, pleading.

I tried not to shake. "Is my grandma really in trouble?

Did you really talk to her?"

Adams crossed his heart. "I swear."

I glanced at Vicki.

"I'll help. You can count on me," she said.

I nodded too. I was convinced. "Yeah, of course. She's my grandma."

* * *

Mum was waiting in the car with a lot of new For Sale signs to put up in front of houses around town. Nobody was buying, though. "Sorry about the mix up. I was so sure about that text from the school. I don't know how I went to the wrong address. I checked five times. I'm so glad you're okay. Hope you weren't too bored."

Vicki and I looked at each other. "No, we weren't bored," I said. It was a good thing Mum got the address wrong.

I should have been all excited about seeing ghosts, but I kept thinking about Grandma. My stomach did spins and my mouth was dry. I couldn't stop licking my lips.

What was I going to do?

"Here we are," Mum said. We pulled up in front of the real Dino Barn, a huge new exhibition hall down by the river covered with flags and banners. "Right place this time."

I swallowed and opened my mouth to say something to Mum, but no words came out, just a tiny squeak. I didn't know what to say. If I told her about Grandma she might worry too much. She worried all the time anyway about Dad being out of work and about money. And what if she thought I was crazy. That would be even more to worry about.

"Have fun," she said.

"Okay. I will."

* * *

After we went inside, Vicki found our class and we joined the group. Children ran back and forth screaming about dinosaurs. I leaned against a wall and imagined all kinds of horrible places Grandma might be. All those scary haunted houses or rat-filled dungeons and bottomless pits I read about spun through my head on a wheel of horror. I always counted on Grandma to tell me things would be okay, but this time she was the one in trouble. I didn't know what to do.

"There you are," Luke said. He raced up and slugged my shoulder. He was wearing a Dino Barn hat and playing with his gooey dino poo. "You're missing out."

Luke dragged me along and we spent the rest of the morning looking at the dino robots and fossil exhibits. Luckily this sneak peek before the grand opening was a bit late getting started, so I hadn't missed much. There were dinosaur skeleton displays everywhere and even a rollercoaster on the inside, the Tyrannosaurus Flex, which, of course, cost too much for me to go on. Luke had money but didn't seem to care.

"Wow!" Luke said. "Look, it's real fossil dinosaur poo. I need some of that."

I checked out the source of Luke's excitement. A chunk of stony stuff the size of a football and shaped like soft ice cream – it even had a little curl on top – sat in a gigantic glass case under a spotlight. Little insects floated just beneath the surface of the poo, and prehistoric flies were glued to the outside. "That's a really big display for some poo."

"It's really big poo." Luke's eyes glowed.

"It's called a coprolite." Vicki had decided to walk around with me now that we were on a secret mission. "From an apatosaurus. They ate mainly plants. And those flies are fake." She was still an annoying know-it-all.

"You would know," Luke said. "You're such a big poo yourself." He held up his glob of fake dinosaur poo and shook it at Vicki.

"Luke!" Mr Brakenbush yelled from across the room.

Luke slipped his goop back into his pocket. "This trip is no fun."

Just then, green, red and blue lights flashed on and off and swirled around the room. Music blared from overhead speakers, drums pounding and horns blowing. A big spotlight pointed a beam at the middle of a stage set up near the triceratops robot and a tall man with wild hair, a moustache the size of my arm and a blinking suit covered with dinosaurs stepped into the circle of light.

Grabbing a microphone he shouted, "Dino Barn, Dino Barn, it's not the farm, it's Dino Barn! Welcome to the brand new Dino Barn, ladies and gentlemen. I'm

Rex Rangler, and I hope you're all enjoying your visit."
He clapped his hands into the mic so it echoed through
the speakers.

Rex Rangler! Wow, there he was. My biggest hero in
person. This should have been cool, but I couldn't forget
about Grandma.

Vicki glared at him, probably imagining him tearing
down old houses.

My whole class gathered around the stage along with
the pupils from a couple of other schools who were there
too. Everyone except Luke, who stayed and stared at
the poo.

"These fearful monsters of the past," Rangler said,
waving his hands at the robots, "are brought to life
for your enjoyment and edification." He winked and
twirled his moustache at Ms Warful, the new Year-6
teacher standing at the front of the crowd. "Marvel at
the triceratops and his menacing horns and impervious
armour as he fends off all attackers. Thrill to the mighty
roar and vicious teeth of Tyrannosaurus rex, king of the
dinosaurs and master of the earth 65 million years ago, a
dark and distant age before the arrival of man."

As he talked the robots sprang to life, spewing steam and roaring above the noise of the crowd. The triceratops ducked its head and lashed out with its horns at the tyrannosaurus, which dodged the strike and plunged its teeth into the triceratops's neck. Everyone cheered or screamed as a fountain of fake blood shot into the air; everyone, that is, except for Luke, who was still looking at poo.

"Fun, eh?" Rangler said. "Unless you're that triceratops. But the Dino Barn is just the beginning of Rangler Enterprises' massive new project that will completely remake our fair city of Townborough. Dino Barn, the new Old-Town Shopping Centre, and next up . . ." The drums rolled again and a curtain lifted behind him to show a giant screen displaying a video of an old-looking mansion with a creaky porch and sagging roof. A big, black orb, looking like a witch's cauldron with the lid on, smoked and steamed behind a grimy window. Bats flitted in and out of the picture and a vulture perched on the porch roof. A black cat squatted on the steps. The house was surrounded by gnarled old trees and an iron gate with spikes on top. He was renewing the city with a crumbling mansion? We had tonnes of those already. Mum was putting For Sale signs up in front of them.

"Next up is Ghostville!" Rangler said. "This haunted house-museum promises to be as big a tourist attraction as the Dino Barn and part of the same gigantic complex. The two will provide a dual look into our past and a vital cog in the economic revival of our fair city. Visitors will see the old buildings from town, carefully recreated here on the site, and be regaled with stories of ghosts, apparitions and poltergeists; spooks and spirits; phantoms, ghouls and spectres. Tourists will flock from all over the world to see our dinosaurs and ghosts, and together they will be the cultural and entertainment centre of the north-east!"

I grabbed Vicki's arm as she spun to look at me.

"Did you hear that?" I asked. "Ghostville. He's tearing down old buildings to make a haunted house."

"I knew my Historic Buildings petition was a good idea," Vicki said.

"Not that. And it's not a good idea, unless you want to lick your own envelopes."

Vicki glared at me. "My dad taught me about history

and those old buildings. They're our link with this town's past . . ."

"I'm talking about Ghostville." I cut off her broken record. "Rex Rangler. Ghosts. Don't you get it? He can help us. He knows all about ghosts. He's even building a gigantic haunted house. Who better to help us rescue my grandma and find the ghostnapper? It's perfect. Why didn't I think of it before?"

Vicki frowned. "I'm not sure. There's something funny about all this."

"Oh, Dan!" Luke cut in and slapped me on the shoulder. "Look at that man's suit. That's so amazing. I wonder if I could get one like that. And Ghostville, even more amazing."

"I know," I said. "Rex Rangler is way cooler than I ever thought. A ghost museum right here in town!"

"You should've done it first," Luke said. "You're the one with the plasmo-blinker."

"Ecto-meter," Vicki said.

Luke looked at her like she'd just landed from the planet Mars. "Doesn't she have a home?"

"That's what it's called," I said. "An ecto-meter."

"Whatever." Luke turned back to Rangler's flashing suit.

I punched Luke in his shoulder and then looked at Rangler. "I need to talk to him about ghosts."

"Let's try." In a flash Vicki's hand was up and she was umming and ohhing like she needed to wee really badly. "Mr Rangler? Can I ask a question?"

Rangler's moustache drooped as he pulled his head out of the tyrannosaurus' mouth. "Why of course, my dear. Ask away."

Vicki glanced at me out of the corner of her eye. "Do you have real ghosts at Ghostville?"

"What?" I whispered in her ear. "What does that have to do with anything?"

Rangler frowned behind his moustache for a moment, and then grinned. "Well, that's kind of a trade secret, young lady. That's the fun of coming to Ghostville, finding out for yourself if the ghosts are real. Who here believes in ghosts?" he asked the crowd. A cheer went up from most of the children. "Then come to Ghostville. Tell your friends, tell your neighbours, tell your neighbour's friends, and learn if ghosts are real."

Vicki shook her head. "I don't think he really knows anything about ghosts. He just turned my question into an advertisement. He can't help us."

"You just asked the wrong question." I raised my hand, too. "Mr Rangler, Mr Rangler. I have a question."

Rangler stared at me, then winked and turned on the flashing lights on his suit. They ran in both directions, circling the dinosaurs and meeting in the middle.

"Come by Ghostville and learn the secrets of the afterworld firsthand." He smiled, but at the same time he jerked his head. A couple of men in sunglasses standing by the edge of the stage nodded. They made their way through the crowd towards us.

"What's the problem?" Vicki asked a guard towering over her. "Did we do something wrong?"

The man with the dark glasses stared over her head. "You ask a lot of questions."

"We're at school. We're supposed to ask questions."

"Don't get wise with me," he said. "I think it's time for you to go."

Vicki backed off. I didn't get the hint. "But I need to talk to Mr Rangler."

"Mr Rangler isn't seeing anyone, especially not nosy children. He's a busy man."

"But . . ."

The guard grabbed my sleeve and pulled me over towards Mr Brakenbush. "Is this boy yours?"

"Dan, what did you and Luke do now?" Mr Brakenbush crossed his arms and stared at us.

"Nothing. I just wanted to ask a question."

"He was bothering Mr Rangler," the guard said. "Please keep your pupils under control."

As the guard let go and walked off, Mr Brakenbush flared his nose at me. "What am I going to do with you, Dan?" He shook his head. "I should have left you at school."

"But . . ."

"No buts. I see many envelopes in your future."

My tongue dried up. How was I going to help Grandma now?

Suddenly Vicki cut in. "It's not like that, Mr Brakenbush. Dan just wanted to ask about ghosts and the guard got all upset for no reason. It wasn't his fault."

Mr Brakenbush looked at Vicki, then at me, then

back and forth. "All right. Dan, you're off the hook this time. But you better be careful from now on." He shook his finger in my face.

"I will."

"Thanks for saving me from detention," I said to Vicki as Mr Brakenbush herded the class back out of the building. I wouldn't have to sit in the head teacher's office, but I'd missed my chance to ask Rex Rangler to help me find Grandma.

CHAPTER EIGHT

DAD'S NEW JOB

After school I rode my bike home and sat in my bedroom staring at my ecto-meter. It was Friday and Mr Brakenbush had given it back at the end of the day. I wondered if that was because of Vicki too. I had to admit that she was becoming kind of helpful.

I closed my eyes and tried to control the hurricane racing through my head. Learning about Grandma's ghost brought back that horrible week two years ago. One day Grandma came down with a terrible headache and she called Mum to take her to the hospital. I wanted to visit, but Mum told me Grandma needed her rest. On the third day Mum came from the hospital and I begged her to take me after school. I started to shiver as she hid her tears. Grandma wasn't coming home. I crawled under my bed with my books and didn't come out until the funeral. But I was too scared to go inside the church. I sat outside in the car by myself, pretending Grandma was there to hold my hand. I never said goodbye.

Grandma was always there for me when I needed her. On my very first day of school I took the bus home, but a huge dog at the bus stop barked at me and Luke. Luke ran one way and the dog chased me the other. I hid in someone's garage until the dog left, but I couldn't find my way home. I sat behind a car, shivering and hugging my knees, wondering how long I had before the dog ate me. Then I heard a voice calling for me. Grandma came and gave me a big hug and walked me home. She said she was really scared, but that she felt better because I was so brave.

"I'll find you, Grandma. I promise."

I kept wondering if I should tell Mum and Dad. They were always so preoccupied with money and jobs. They didn't say anything about it while I was around, but at night after I went to bed I could hear them talking. Maybe they thought I didn't know, but it was hard to hide. I'd asked Dad about jobs a few times, but he just told me not to worry.

I decided to give it a try at dinner anyway.

"Um, Mum?" I asked while wiping rice off my face. Ever since Dad had lost his job we ate some kind of rice thing almost every night. Dad and I both had little pieces stuck to our chins. "You know that programme I like, *Spirit Trackers*? Well, see, they're opening this new Ghostville place next to the Dino Barn and . . ."

"Not just yet, dear," Mum said. "Your dad has a big announcement. Go ahead, dear."

This was weird. Dad used to tell jokes and be all funny at dinner, but since he lost his job he mainly ate in silence. He brushed off a chunk of rice and cleared his throat. He had a big smile. "Speaking of Ghostville, I heard about it. Sounded really interesting."

"Really?" I said. "Cause I think that the owner . . ."

"Rex Rangler," Dad said. "He's got ideas. Real mover and shaker. Terrific person to be connected with."

"Yeah. That's why I want to talk to . . ."

He cut in again. "As a matter of fact, you're looking at Ghostville's newest employee."

Mum jumped up and hugged Dad across the table. "That's so wonderful. When do you start?"

"Ghostville's opening in the next two weeks. So there's plenty of set-up to do. I'll be driving a lorry and moving things from tomorrow."

"It must feel so good." Mum grinned like it was Christmas morning.

"It does," Dad said. "It really does. Now maybe we can afford more than rice every night. What do you think of that, Dan?" He held up his hand for a fist-bump. I tapped his knuckles. "Maybe we'll go out for burgers tomorrow to celebrate. How's that sound?"

"Great." We hadn't gone out in months, not even for ice cream.

"Or maybe pizza. Would you like that better?"

"Burgers, pizza, whatever."

"Great, pizza it is."

"Um, Dad, do you know Rex Rangler? Because I need to ask him . . ."

Dad shook his head. "Can't do that. Mr Rangler is a very private person, very busy. We were warned not to bother him with any problems. I heard a couple of people got sacked just for talking to him. Plus there are those guards around him all the time. Pretty touchy. I suppose that's the way those TV stars live, though. Too big for the little people like us." He grinned. "But as long as I get paid, makes no difference to me."

My heart dropped. Dad had been looking for a job since last year when they closed the bottling plant. Every night he came home from searching for work, flopped into his chair and stared at the wall. We hardly ever played catch anymore. He was too busy checking the job ads online. Mum tried to show as many houses as possible, but no one was buying. I couldn't get him in trouble at his new job. I was going to have to find Grandma on my own.

Dinner didn't look good anymore, so I pulled out my ecto-meter. I scrolled through all my old readings. It was a pretty short list. Except for the Vicki sighting in the toilets there was only that same error code, a series of six numbers. I'd got them four times since Mr Brakenbush took the meter away. I wished I could have tested it on Adams.

Stupid ecto-meter. Why couldn't it just light up and tell me where Grandma was?

"Dan, please don't play with that at the table," Mum said. I tucked the meter back in my pocket as she squinted at me. "What's the matter? Not hungry? Sorry we don't have pizza tonight, but I've got rice pudding for dessert."

"I think I'll just go to my room." That was dumb. Mum was bound to know something was wrong. Rice pudding might be made out of rice, but it was still pudding, and I never turned down pudding.

"I've never seen you skip dessert before," she said. "Is there something you want to talk about?"

"No, I'm okay. Just not hungry."

Mum reached over and put her hand on my head. "You're not getting sick are you?"

"No, Mum, I'm fine."

"Let me get the torch."

Every time Mum thought I was ill she stuck a light down my throat to look for disease. Grandma used to do the same thing, but she always said she was looking for ghosts in my mouth. Mum went to the kitchen drawer, pulled out a torch and turned it on. "Open up." She aimed the beam towards my innards.

I stuck out my tongue. "Aaaahhhhhhh."

"I don't see anything." Mum pulled down my right eyelid, looking for ooze or terminal redness. "But you're pale as a ghost. Maybe you should go to bed."

I didn't want to say anything. Everyone was happy

for once, so I just smiled and faked it. "I'm not ill. Seriously. I just have homework." That sounded even more stupid. If I didn't shut up, Mum would have me in hospital next.

I got up and put my plate in the sink, then dashed upstairs to my room and closed the door. I dived on my bed and hid under the pillow. I didn't know what else to do.

A couple of minutes later Mum knocked. She opened the door and peeked in. She held an armful of books.

"Can I come in?" she asked. I pulled my head out from under the pillow and nodded. She sat next to me on the bed. "I haven't read to you in a long time, but I remember how much you loved it when Grandma read you stories. These were from her house."

I stared up at the ceiling. "Mum, where do you think she is?"

Mum leaned over and kissed the top of my head. "Well, your grandma is in a better place, a place where she doesn't have any more worries. A place where she's happy."

"Do you think she remembers us, or misses us?"

"I'm sure she does. She loved you very much. I know I miss her every day."

I glanced at the books. They were mainly little kid books, but one was a collection of ghost stories for older children. *Spook's Bones* was my favourite. It was the first story I ever read on my own, but Grandma also read it to me a hundred times. "I want that one."

It was about two boys who meet a ghost and dig up, then rebury, his bones so he can find peace and stop haunting the room above their garage. When Grandma first read it to me, I was kind of scared, but later it was just fun. Dad made me fill in all the holes I dug in the garden looking for skeletons.

Mum read a few pages, but then I started to feel silly. "I'm kind of old to be read to."

"You're never too old," Mum said, ruffling my hair. "I'll leave the book if you want to read it yourself." She got up, stopping by my desk to blow dust off my model aeroplanes. "Things are going to be better. Your dad has a new job. You don't have to worry so much."

I wanted to tell her my real worries but my mouth overruled my brain.

"Thanks, Mum."

After she left I called Luke and told him to meet me the next morning so we could look for ghosts. But Luke wasn't enough. I needed someone else, too.

I stared at the phone wondering if I should. My hand got all sweaty and my heart raced. Why was this such a big deal? It was just a phone call. Vicki had offered to help, and she already knew the whole ghost story. But I'd never called a girl before. Would it sound weird? What if her mum or dad answered? What was Luke going to say if I brought someone else along to help, especially someone he didn't like except to tease?

I flipped open *Spook's Bones* again and looked through some of the pictures of the children talking to the ghost. After ten minutes I took a deep breath and dialled the number.

I was still listening to my heart thump when someone picked up on the first ring. "Hello?"

I was glad it sounded like Vicki and not her mum or

dad. I didn't want to explain who I was and why I was calling. "Vicki?"

"Yes, this is Vicki. Who's calling?"

"Hi, this is uh . . . this is Dan. You know, from school."

"Oh, hi, Dan! Of course I know. I just saw you three hours ago." She sounded giggly. "What's going on?"

"Can you come . . . can you help me find my grandma tomorrow?"

"Of course. I was hoping you'd ask me. I'm totally excited to find your grandma."

Wow. Calling a girl was much easier than I thought it would be. Why was I all sweaty?

"I'll have to ask my mum," Vicki said. "She doesn't like me . . . uh . . ."

"She doesn't like you talking to boys?" I asked.

Vicki giggled again, a bit nervously. "No, she doesn't like me talking about ghosts. I'll just tell her we're getting together. I'm sure it will be okay."

"I didn't tell my mum or dad either. They don't mind if I talk about ghosts, but I don't know what to say . . . you know."

"I get it. My mum doesn't want to be reminded of . . ."

Vicki went silent. Did she hang up on me?

"Vicki? Are you still there?"

"Yeah," she said after a few seconds, her voice catching.

"What happened? Did your mum come in?"

"No," she said. "Nothing. Is, uh, is Luke coming?"

"Yeah. He always comes."

Vicki went quiet again. I was sure she didn't like Luke any more than he liked her. "Don't worry, he's okay. Are you still coming?"

"Totally."

It was a good thing I hadn't told Luke about Vicki coming. He might bring spiders and jam.

"Do you have a plan?" she asked after a few more seconds.

"Sort of. I'll tell you tomorrow."

"Okay, I'll be there." I heard her take a big breath. "Dan, I think it's totally amazing that you're going to rescue your grandma. It's brave. You're really brave."

"Uh, thanks." For some weird reason my heart pounded even harder. "See you tomorrow, about nine o'clock?"

"Nine o'clock. Bye, Dan."

I hung up. I didn't feel brave. I just sat there, wishing Grandma would read *Spook's Bones* to me.

CHAPTER NINE

YES, SHE'S COMING

I was determined to find Grandma's ghostnapper and rescue her, but I needed help. Rex Rangler's help. It wasn't a genius plan, but it was all I had. Luke, Vicki and I would go back to the Dino Barn and try to see him again. I just had to make sure he didn't know who I was or that Dad worked for him.

I didn't want to lie, so I told my parents that we were looking for ghosts, just not which one.

"Ghosts?" Dad said, shaking his head as he downed the last of the milk right out of the carton. I suppose I'd have to eat dry Rice Puffs. "We need to find you a better hobby. You know ghosts aren't real, don't you?"

"But you're working at Ghostville," I said.

"It's just a job. They don't really have ghosts there."

"Well, there's a £10,000 prize on *Spirit Trackers* for finding a ghost."

"I suppose it can't hurt," he said with a wink. "And it's pretty harmless."

Dad was always convinced by prizes – prizes with money.

"Can't get into trouble looking for ghosts." Dad brushed at a spot that had dribbled from the carton onto his jacket. "Don't tell your mum," he said, grinning. "She'll want me to wash it." He squeezed my shoulder and headed out the door. That's the kind of job I want – one where you can go to work with milk on your clothes.

I waited outside on my bike. Luke showed up first, wolfing down a bag of crisps. I never saw him carrying any food, but he always magically made something salty or sugary appear out of nowhere. He was a junk food wizard.

Vicki arrived a minute later on her purple bike with red and yellow flames, wearing a helmet and a *Spelling Bee Championship* backpack. I remembered that contest. I misspelled *obtuse*. I still don't know what it means.

"I brought a lunch." She shook her bag and chewed on some bubblegum.

I hoped the mention of food would catch Luke's ear, but instead he just stared at me, his mouth hanging open. "What's she doing here?" he finally said.

"Vicki's coming," I said.

Luke just kept on staring. "No way," he said.

Vicki looked away, hiding her face.

"This is our thing," Luke said. "Just you and me."

"Vicki's coming too. She knows about ghosts." My stomach rolled over and I glanced at Vicki. The more I thought about it, the more I realized that I didn't really know her. She'd only been in my class since September and I think she was new to the school, too. She raised her hand a lot and answered loads of questions and set up mailing campaigns and never got into trouble, but before getting stuck with her yesterday, I hadn't ever talked to her alone. I wondered for a moment why I had asked her to come.

Luke's face darkened and he squeezed his handlebars. Vicki wobbled back and forth on her bike. "Come on man," I said to Luke. "What's the problem?"

Luke gritted his teeth. "What's wrong with you? Ghosts are our deal, you and me. Hunting ghosts is for boys, and *she's* a *girl*."

"That's stupid," Vicki said, finally speaking. "I'm the one who first recognized the ghosts."

"She's good at finding clues, too," I said, trying to convince myself as much as Luke. Why couldn't Luke make this easy?

He kicked at the ground and slapped his handlebars. "Don't ask me to hold your hand when you get scared."

"Don't worry," Vicki said. "I'll punch you if you touch me."

★ ★ ★

The Dino Barn wasn't very close and it took us nearly half an hour to get there. The car park was full for the sneak-peek grand-opening weekend. People streamed in to see the dino robots eat each other and marvel at gigantic piles of fossilized poo. The queues went on forever. We pulled up behind the crowd near the fence to look things over.

"How are we going to find Rangler in all of this?" I asked.

"We'll just have to queue," Vicki said. "But I really think we should be looking on our own. From what I heard yesterday, Rex Rangler doesn't know a ghost from a coprolite. He can't help us."

"That's the only idea I have. If Rangler doesn't know, then I'm stuck."

"Dan." A light came on in Luke's eyes. "I thought we were going to find our own ghosts. These are Rangler's."

Vicki shook her head and put her hands on her hips. "Ghosts aren't anybody's, they belong to themselves. Dan and I are trying to set them free, not capture our own."

"Who asked you?" Luke looked at me. "What is she talking about?"

I realized it was time to tell Luke what was going on.

"She's helping me find my grandma."

"Your grandma's dead," Luke said.

"I know – it's her ghost that's missing."

"What?! Your grandma's a ghost? That is so cool! Where is she?"

"That's why we're here." I told him the story about meeting Adams and how I thought Rangler might know how to find her.

"Wow, this is going to be cool. Ghost rescue. But I still don't know why we need her."

He looked over his shoulder at Vicki.

"We just do. She's helping." I glanced at Vicki, but she was looking at her feet.

Luke turned to Vicki and pulled on her backpack. "What's for lunch?"

Vicki pulled back her bag and hugged it. "Some sandwiches, crisps, apples and cartons of juice. But it's not time to eat yet. We have to find the ghosts first."

"How come?" Luke asked. "I'm hungry now. Are you saving some for the ghosts? 'Cause they don't eat. I thought you were supposed to be clever."

"Let's just go and find Rex Rangler." I pulled out my ecto-meter. It was easier dealing with my equipment than arguing with Luke.

Beep, beep, beep. Only a thin green line, flat and straight, and those stupid error codes. It was Rangler or nothing.

"How does that work?" Vicki leaned over on her bike, taking a closer look. Most people weren't interested. Okay, no one was interested, not even Luke. He thought it was a video game.

"Well," I said, "it's not working at the moment. But this green line here is supposed to bounce up and down in the presence of ectoplasmic disturbances. No ectoplasm, no ghost. Most ghosts don't just come up and talk to you like Adams."

Vicki frowned. "Especially the kidnapped ones." She poked at the screen. "Does that have an infrared emanation detector like the Spectre-Seeker 3000? Sometimes ghosts don't give off detectable levels of ectoplasm, but can still be seen on the infrared level."

Wow! How did she know that?

"You've heard of a Spectre-Seeker 3000?"

"Of course," she said. "I think it's the best detector, but it is kind of expensive. Did you say you made your own? That's pretty cool."

"Yeah," I said, "it wasn't that hard. Basically I just put the ectoplasm detector chip I ordered online into the memory card slot of this old mobile phone. I got the plans online, too. Now it's supposed to show ghosts instead of phone numbers."

"Cool," Vicki said.

"I didn't know you were into ghosts, not until yesterday anyway. How come you never said?"

Vicki looked down at her feet again and dug her toe

into the pavement. "You lot always make fun of me. I know you don't like me."

"That's true," Luke said, butting in. "*Nobody* likes you. Now are you two going to get married, or can I eat?"

Vicki's face scrunched and she narrowed her eyes. She pulled a sandwich out of her bag and threw it at Luke's head. It bounced off his ear and into the gutter where he scrambled after it, wiping mud off the plastic bag. Then Vicki tossed her bag over her shoulder and pedalled off.

"Find your own ghosts!"

CHAPTER TEN

ON MY OWN?

I watched Vicki ride away from the Dino Barn car park. She was steaming mad at Luke for teasing her, and I wasn't too happy either. I told myself it would be okay. After all, I only wanted to talk to Rangler about helping me find Grandma. I hoped Luke wouldn't mess that up too.

"Peanut butter?" Luke said, stuffing half a sandwich in his mouth all at once. "That's all she brought?" Crumbs sprayed everywhere when he talked. "I need some mayo. Oh, well, at least she's gone." He hiccupped hard enough to cause an earthquake. "Better get something to drink. Want to go to the chip shop?"

"No, I told you I have to find my grandma. Didn't you understand? Her ghost has been kidnapped!"

"All right." Luke held up his hands, still hiccupping. "I'm going to help. But that queue will take forever. I need a drink." He jumped back on his bike.

"You're leaving?"

"Yeah, I just said."

"What's wrong with you? I have to help my grandma!"

He rolled his eyes. "Me too, but I'm choking on that sandwich. Want something?"

"No!"

Luke cycled off and left me alone. I couldn't believe it. It was bad enough Vicki ran away whenever someone called her a name, but Luke was supposed to be my friend. We did everything together. When Dad stopped me from digging up pretend skeletons, we tore up Luke's lawn instead. We built model aeroplanes, played video games, rugby and cricket together. I even broke Luke's arm playing football three years ago. I spent so much time with him that Mum never noticed when he was there for dinner. He did kind of stop coming when we switched to a mostly rice diet, but I still ate at his house a lot.

As Luke rode away I sat down on the kerb, kicking the loose gravel. My head steamed. I wanted to punch something. I couldn't count on anyone. I checked my ecto-meter again. Still a straight green line.

Stupid piece of junk! Didn't anything work?

Then for just a moment I thought the line wavered a tiny bit at one edge. I stared hard and blinked and rubbed my eyes. The line was straight again. I must have imagined it. I'd never find a ghost with this thing.

I thought about Grandma, probably held prisoner in some terrible pit or dungeon by a demon or something. Now that I knew she was still a person and not just some ectoplasm I wondered if she was scared. She was probably all alone without any friends, like me. Rex Rangler was my only hope. I looked up at the people going inside the Dino Barn. It looked like there were a million of them and it didn't look like I was going to be able to jump the queue. I stared back down at my shoes. This was never going to work.

"Where are you Grandma?" I whispered.

A pair of tyres skidded to a halt right next to me. "Back already?" I asked Luke without looking up. "That was fast." I wondered why I didn't get splashed with his drink. He usually hit me with the overflow.

"I saw Luke leave without you, so I came back. How come you spend time with him? He's kind of mean."

I looked up to see Vicki pulling off her bike helmet

and running her fingers through her hair. I wasn't sure anymore.

"He's my best friend," I said, shrugging.

Vicki nodded. "Yeah. You're lucky to have a best friend."

"Lucky? He left to get a drink."

Vicki hopped off her bike and stood over me. "Dan?" She took a deep breath. "Can I ask you something?"

"I've known Luke since we were little," I said. "He's usually not such a pain."

"Not that. When . . . when did your grandma die?"

I jerked my head up. I'd expected her to complain more about Luke. Now I just felt a rock in my gut. "Two years ago."

"What happened?"

"She had a stroke." I turned away. Even saying the word "stroke" made my eyes wet.

"I'm sorry," Vicki said. "Were you there?"

"I don't want to talk about it."

"That's okay. I understand. I was just wondering, you know, what it was like." As Vicki looked at me, her eyes swelled up like balloons and her lips quivered.

I didn't know why she was so interested. I didn't know why I was telling her. I'd never really talked about it to anyone before.

"I . . . I wasn't there. I wanted to visit the hospital, but it was too late."

Vicki closed her eyes for a moment. "Oh. Do you miss her a lot?"

I nodded. "Yeah, I supoose so. I mean . . . yeah."

"It's hard, isn't it? Losing someone you love so much. Makes you feel kind of lost."

"Sort of. Why do you want to know?"

"It's just . . ." Vicki stopped and stared off into the distance for a minute.

I'd hidden in my room for months after Grandma's funeral, telling myself that she was just an old woman and it didn't matter that she was gone. But I never believed it. Now I'd do anything to get her back.

Vicki cracked a small smile. "Should we see if we can find Rangler?"

"Yeah." I jumped off the kerb. Finally I could do something. My head ached from talking about feelings.

★ ★ ★

I glanced again at the queue of people waiting to get in, buying Dino Barn T-shirts, hats and candy floss. With Vicki here it didn't look like so many people. But there was another problem. Yesterday had been free, but today – I should have thought of this before. "Do you have any money for a ticket?"

Vicki dug through her backpack and pulled out a handful of change, not even enough for a drink. "I spent my pocket money on petitions."

"Why are you so into those things?"

"My dad taught me to stand up for what I believe in. That's what he always did."

I nodded. I suppose that made sense. I searched my pockets too, one pound fifty, all of my pocket money. One thing Luke usually carried was plenty of money.

"We'll have to sneak in," I said.

Vicki grinned. "I've never been in trouble before. It sounds like fun."

"We might run into those security guards." This worried me. That one man had a pretty strong grip.

"Well, it sounds like fun anyway. Let's go."

Her eyes lit up. "Your grandma needs you."

After chaining our bikes against a fence, we made our way around the back of the building on the river side. The Dino Barn didn't look that big from the front because it was dug into a small hill, but walking around it I thought it would never end. There was a path lined with trees that curved around the building leading to a back entrance. A trench cut through the path and workers in yellow vests and helmets jumped in and out of the hole. We skirted around the work and I looked for an opening where we wouldn't attract attention. I tried a couple of doors but they were all locked and had security pads.

"You don't know how to break key codes, do you?" I punched in a couple of numbers but only got a sharp *buzzzzzz*.

Vicki shook her head and popped some gum in her mouth, her cheeks bulging. She was as dainty an eater as Luke. "No, but there's the loading dock." She pointed to a big garage-like opening. "It's open."

A lorry was parked at the edge of the dock and a man in a blue jacket with a *Rangler Enterprises* patch on the back unloaded boxes. He had milk down his front.

Dad said he was starting work today. I grabbed Vicki and pulled her back around the corner of the building behind a shrub. I didn't tell her that I knew the driver.

"Don't let him see us," I said.

"It's only a lorry driver. He won't do anything. We're just two children hanging out at the grand opening."

"No, we're not. We're sneaking in, remember?"

Vicki shrugged and we waited for Dad to drive off.

"What did you tell your mum you were doing?" I asked Vicki while we waited.

She shrugged. "Just that I was going to a friend's house. She wanted to know what friend, so I gave her your number. She might call your mum, so you can say we went for a bike ride or something. Your mum knows me anyway."

"Yeah." I hoped I wouldn't have to answer a million questions about spending time with a girl and not Luke. I had enough to worry about.

As I watched, Dad unloaded one more thing from the lorry, a small crate he left sitting on the dock. "Does your dad care if you look for ghosts like your mum does?"

Vicki glanced away. "No. But he's not around."

"I thought he took you to old films and wrote your petitions?"

Vicki shook her head.

"You know Luke's dad left too. He moved to Ireland when we were eight. For a long time I thought it was my fault because he was so mad when Luke and I dug up his garden looking for skeletons."

Vicki seemed to have stopped listening to me. Luke didn't like to talk about his dad either. "I wonder what that crate is," she said, changing the subject after Dad drove off.

"Dinosaur egg?"

Vicki pursed her lips, still chewing. "Too big."

"Giant dino poo?"

"Not heavy enough. That thing only took one person to carry. Petrified poo weighs a lot. It's rock, you know."

"Yes, I know. Dinosaurs pooed rock. I get it."

Vicki's eyes rolled. "They didn't poo rock; it turned into rock later. That's what petrified means."

"It's not what dinosaurs ate?"

Vicki slapped her forehead and glared at me with one eye half closed. I was giving her brain damage.

"Gotcha." I laughed. "I'm not that dumb. Dinosaurs ate mud, and that hardened into rock. Now let's go and find Rex Rangler."

I crept off before Vicki could sigh me to death. Keeping low, I made my way alongside the back wall of the building to the edge of the dock. I peeked over the lip with one eye to see if the coast was clear. "Nobody here," I said in a whisper. "I don't see any security guards or workers. Just that package. Let's go."

I jumped up on the dock and crouched low, crab walking behind the crate. Vicki inched in beside me.

"I think we're okay," I said. "No one saw us."

Just then the crate jiggled back and forth, rattling on the concrete.

"Did you see that?" I asked.

"What? Is somebody there?"

I poked at the crate. "No, in here. It moved."

Vicki leaned in to get a better look, shaking her head. "You probably bumped it."

I knew I hadn't touched it before, but I decided to now. Up close I could see inside through the slats. Whatever was moving looked black and round like a bowling ball.

It reminded me of something I'd seen recently, but I couldn't remember what. Sticking my finger through an opening I gave the thing a poke.

"Weird," I said.

"What?"

"It feels wet."

I poked my finger in again. I jumped away as a blast of greenish steam hissed out. The ball rolled back and forth and banged against the sides of the crate. One corner of the crate split open.

"I think that dinosaur egg is about to hatch."

"Eggs don't give off steam," Vicki said.

"Have you ever seen a dinosaur egg hatch?"

"No, but . . ."

"Ha!"

Vicki scowled, but didn't answer. Score one for me, *Miss Know-it-all*.

I pulled the corner of the crate away to get a better look. The ball was so black it could have been a bottomless pit. I couldn't resist touching it again.

"Careful," Vicki said.

"I know what I'm doing." I plunged my hand in.

It felt like dipping my hand into the washing machine and waiting for it to start spinning. My wrist vanished. I tried to pull it out, but the ball tugged and in a flash my whole arm slipped inside.

The thing was trying to eat me! It had to be a dinosaur egg.

Vicki let out a tiny shriek and grabbed me around the neck. I felt my throat crushing under her grip, but my arm slowly emerged from the ball as she pulled. A second later I shot free, flopping onto my back.

I bolted up and checked my arm to make sure everything had made it out okay. Five fingers, so I hadn't been eaten.

Beep, beep, beeeeeeep. My ecto-meter! The screen flashed like a lightning storm, and it was ringing. A message popped onto the screen.

Vicki leaned over my shoulder. "Are you getting a signal?"

"Yeah," I said. "It's a message."

"A message? From who?"

"I don't know."

We both watched as the message scrolled out, one letter at a time.

H-E-L-P.

CHAPTER ELEVEN

IT WORKS!

Vicki and I sat on the Dino Barn loading dock, both staring at the green line on my ecto-meter as it jumped up and down across the screen. Just below it a message ran, spelling the same word over and over.

H-E-L-P--H-E-L-P--H-E-L-P--H-E-L-P--H-E-L-P

"It works!" I pumped my fist. "My ecto-meter works! The ghosts are in there."

"Inside that thing?" Vicki gasped, leaning in for a closer look at the steaming bowling ball. She squinted and stuck her finger out, but didn't touch it. "Let me see your ecto-meter."

I handed it to her and she pushed some buttons.

"Don't lose the signal," I said, watching her fiddle with the controls. "Ectoplasm dissipates pretty fast."

"It's showing a number now: 599789? What's that mean?"

"That shows up all the time. It's an error code. It's the wavy line that's important, and the message."

"Looks like a phone number to me," Vicki said. "Isn't this just an old phone with an ectoplasmic chip stuffed into it?"

"No. Maybe. So?"

"So somebody's texting you."

She handed the ecto-meter back and I gave it a shake. Not again. Did Vicki always have to be right? I gave it another look. A lump rose in my throat. I'd seen that same number over and over, but now I finally recognized it. It was Grandma's old phone number.

How could I have missed that? All this time she was trying to contact me and I didn't know. A pit grew in my stomach. How much time had I wasted?

"It's from my grandma. That's her number! She's in there! We have to get her out." My heart thundered like a jet.

Vicki stared at the black hole, frowning. "Dan, if you're right, do you know what this means?"

"It means we have to get my grandma out of this ball."

I'd found her, and I couldn't wait any longer. I was going to see Grandma again! I was really going to see her, just like when she was alive. "Come on, help me pry it open." I reached over to wrestle the rest of the crate away.

"Wait." Vicki pulled my hand back. "Of course we have to save your grandma. But it means something else. It also means that Rex Rangler is the ghostnapper."

I froze. "What? That can't be true. He's a good guy."

Vicki shook her head. "It all makes sense. He's tearing down those old haunted buildings like the cinema, paving over the cemetery and building a ghost museum. It has to be him. He's putting real ghosts into Ghostville."

I didn't believe her. Rex was my favourite TV presenter, my hero. My dad's boss. It couldn't be him.

"You're just saying that because you don't like him. Because he's tearing down those old houses you love."

But I loved them too. At least one. Grandma's house.

"Think about it, Dan. Why would this thing be here if it wasn't Rangler's?"

"Maybe he doesn't know," I said. "Maybe he thinks like I did, that ghosts are just ectoplasmic remnants and not real people."

"Maybe," Vicki said. "But he's still the one kidnapping them."

My head hurt. I couldn't just sit here and argue. I had to do something. I pulled the rest of the crate apart and leaned in over the ball. It steamed and wiggled.

"What are you doing? Don't get too close. It might not be safe."

"I have to find out for sure if Grandma is in there."

"No!" Vicki grabbed my arm.

I took a deep breath and shook her loose. Vicki had her petitions, and I had Grandma. "I'm standing up for what *I* believe in." Then I shoved my head into the ball.

The last thing I heard was Vicki shouting, "Why don't you return the message?"

Now she tells me.

* * *

At first everything went black. I had fallen into a bottomless pit. Then I thought I might be in outer space, except there were no stars. My skin crawled as I tumbled head over heels. I couldn't tell up from down. I was moving so fast I had to be billions of kilometres away, falling through a portal into another universe.

My head spun like a top and my stomach jumped into

my mouth. After what seemed like hours, the blackness switched to a cloudy grey like the middle of a rain cloud. Then, like opening my eyes in the morning, the fog disappeared and I could see again. I was standing alone on a staircase. I looked around and saw that the steps led up to another staircase that ran in a different direction, upside down. And it connected to more steps running sideways into more stairs which ran into more stairs . . . on and on and on with no end.

I whacked my head on the flight coming down from above. That was sure to leave a bump. Rubbing my wound I crouched down and managed to get to the top without cracking my face again. The weirdest part was when I reached the last stair I flipped over and was standing straight up, but on a connecting staircase. I ran to the bottom and turned upside down again. No matter where I climbed or which steps I took, I always ended up in the place I started. I liked the blackness better.

"Hello?" I called. "Is anybody here? Grandma?"

Out of the blue dozens of fuzzy shapes materialized, misty and glowing like fireflies in smoke. I blinked and the room filled with dozens of people. Some stood around me, their eyes glaring, while others were upside down or at weird angles on different steps. They all stared and pointed.

I tried to back away, but I only switched direction and ended up surrounded by another group of blurry people. They all had a kind of whitish-grey look. Some shimmered and I could see through them to the person behind. They had to be ghosts.

The nearest spirit, a woman in a pink bathrobe, scowled wide-eyed at me. She held a tiny drooling poodle with ribbons dangling from its ears and a bow around its neck. "Why did you bring us here? Foo-Foo doesn't like it here." Foo-Foo snapped and barked. I backed into another ghost. He clawed at me but his fingers passed right through me as if I wasn't there.

I ran and tripped, falling straight through another ghost who'd swung a fist at my head. Stumbling, I dashed down the stairs, passing through every ghost on the way. They all cried out as I zoomed through their insides. But there was no place to go. The stairs all wound back on themselves and the ghosts were everywhere.

Voices called out from all directions, filling my ears

and rattling my teeth. "Let us go! Free us! We want to go home!"

I threw my hands over my ears, but the noise seeped in just like their bodies passed through me. I couldn't get away.

"I didn't bring you here! It wasn't me!"

Dozens of pale fingers pointed their accusations at me. "Where's Adams? What have you done with him?"

"Nothing. He sent me here," I said.

"Let us go!"

No one listened. I hadn't cried to my grandma for help in years, but this seemed like a good time. "Grandma! It's me, Dan! Help!!!"

Just like that the crowd went quiet. The ghosts kept staring, but everyone stopped talking.

"Are you Dan?" the bathrobed woman asked.

I nodded.

Spinning and dropping her dog she cried, "It's him. It's Dan! He's here! Dan's here!" She reached out and put her hand on my face. Her fingers passed right through my nose. "She said you'd come, that you'd help us."

The woman stepped aside and the crowed parted.

A misty shape walked towards me, solidifying until it looked like a woman with curly grey hair and glasses. She smiled big and wide. "Dan, dear. You got my text."

CHAPTER TWELVE

CATCHING UP

Grandma.

I ran up and hugged her. I hadn't seen her in two years and all I wanted was to sit on her lap again and have her read me a story even though I was too big.

I flopped right through her and bounced down the stairs.

"Careful, dear," Grandma said. "I'm not as solid as I used to be." She bent over to help me up, but that didn't work any better than my hug.

She sat down beside me. "Oh, Dan, I'm so glad to see you. I told everyone that my brave boy would come to help us, and here you are. You're looking so grown up."

For some reason, even though I couldn't touch her, Grandma still smelled the same as always. Kind of a mixture of roses and those sticky hard sweets she kept in a bowl that even I couldn't manage to eat.

I had so many questions, but something nagged at me even more.

"I . . . I'm sorry I didn't go to your funeral, Grandma. I . . ." I looked away. She always said I was so brave, so how could I tell her I was too scared to go?

She smiled and tilted her head. "Don't worry about that, Dan. I wasn't there myself."

"Really?"

"Oh heavens no, funerals are no fun. I sat in the car with my grandson, holding his hand. I felt so much braver with your help, just like now."

I remembered that day. I'd thought I'd imagined holding her hand. "You were there?"

"Of course."

"Did it hurt?" I asked. "You know, when you died?"

"Not that I remember. More like falling asleep."

"I'm glad," I said. I didn't want to think she'd suffered. "Who brought you here?" I crossed my fingers and hoped Vicki was wrong and that it wasn't Rangler.

"It was the strangest thing," Grandma said. "I was at home, looking through some old photos after the funeral. Then out of the blue these men burst in, beep-beeping everywhere. The next thing I knew I was trapped here with all these nice people."

I gasped. "They tore your house down a year ago."

Grandma put her hand over her mouth. "Has it been that long? No wonder you look so grown up. I suppose I lost track. Time seems to stand still, and since I'm not getting any older I don't watch the clock too much."

"How did you know I'd come?" I asked. "You . . . you can't see me all the time, can you?" I started worrying that she'd been watching while Luke was getting me into trouble. "'Cause I'm sorry about the glue on the seats."

Grandma smiled. "Don't worry, dear, I only haunted you that once."

That was lucky, because we did the glue thing a lot.

"Who else would I call but my brave grandson?" She smiled and tried to touch my cheek. "You always said you were going to find a real ghost. And I was lucky I had this." She reached into her pocket and pulled out her phone. It looked just like the one I'd transformed into my ecto-meter. We were probably still on the same family plan. "I texted the address to your mum, too, just in case. I'm so glad you finally answered. I haven't paid the bill, so I was a bit worried."

"That's why mum took us to the wrong place," I said.

It made sense now. Grandma had been sending me clues all along. "I talked to Adams. He told me you'd been kidnapped."

"Isn't he a wonderful man? So concerned about all of us."

"He's a bit weird," I said.

Grandma chuckled. "Smokes too much, too. But very nice."

"How can you use that?" I pointed at her phone. "Your hands go right through everything else."

Grandma shrugged. "For some reason we ghosts can use anything we were holding, or wearing, when we died. Luckily it works with clothes, too." She smoothed her trouser suit. "I really hate this thing. It was a present from your mother. I hope they didn't bury me in it."

I looked down at the floor and wondered if she had ever liked my presents. But insects glued to a paper plate are a lot cooler than a green trouser suit. Maybe she could borrow some different clothes as soon as we'd got out of here. That reminded me of something else. With her house torn down, where would she live?

I'd have to take her home with me. Mum had always

wanted her to live with us anyway. And ghosts didn't need that much room, so I was sure Dad wouldn't mind. We'd all be together again. I smiled at my brilliant plan.

"Come on, Grandma. We're leaving." I looked around. I was so excited to see her I'd forgotten that there wasn't any way out, just the stairs to nowhere. I didn't know how to get home any more than the ghosts did.

"We better give this a little more thought." Grandma smiled. "I wouldn't want you to miss any school on my account."

I tried to remember how I'd got here, but that was just a blur. I didn't know if I was inside that ball on the loading dock or in another dimension.

"There's no egress."

Grandma clapped her hands. "Oh my! Egress! What a wonderful word. The things they teach in school these days."

"Actually I learned it— "

Suddenly my middle squeezed like a vice. A tornado swirled around me and I stretched into spaghetti just like Adams. Except he was a ghost and didn't mind.

"Grandma! Help!"

She reached out her hands, but they flowed straight through me. In another second Grandma and the rest of the ghosts shrank in the distance and the blackness returned. Something was pulling me away.

After a minute of flying across the universe, I opened my eyes and shook my head. Wrapped around my waist and staring me straight in the face was a gigantic, monstrous, horrible . . .

"Vicki?"

"Why did you put your head in there? You got stuck. I had to pull you out."

"What do you mean? I was inside this totally other dimension."

"No, you weren't," Vicki said. "You put your face in the ball and sat there for a minute. I heard someone coming, so I pulled you out."

"No way. I saw my grandma. All the ghosts are inside. We have to get them out."

"We'll have to come back later." Vicki tugged on my arm and I followed her jerking head towards a door leading inside the building. The knob turned and the door cracked open. Then the tip of a giant moustache appeared around the edge. Right behind it flashed a dinosaur suit, covered with Christmas lights.

"Run," Vicki whispered.

I took one last look at the black hole and promised Grandma that I'd be back, whatever it took.

CHAPTER THIRTEEN

THE REAL REX RANGLER

We slid off the Dino Barn loading dock, but the door opened all the way before we could run. Crouching below the lip of the dock, I held my breath and waited. Vicki even stopped chewing her bubblegum.

I still couldn't believe Rangler was behind all the ghostnapping. Maybe it wasn't him. Maybe his lackeys wanted to impress him by capturing real ghosts. He was a big TV star, and everyone loves TV stars.

"What's that doing there?" Rangler slapped at a guard on his right, all muscles and hairy arms. He was the same one who'd got me into trouble the day before. "What idiot left that sitting outside in the open?"

Hey! He was talking about my dad!

"Some numbskull leaves our top-secret project on the porch? Morons! I work with morons!"

The guard nodded blankly while he scanned the dock, looking out from behind his sunglasses. "I'll look into it."

"Make sure you do," Rangler said with a sneer. "Or you'll be looking for work. I don't tolerate messes like this. No one else in the world will have real ghosts in their amusement park. Can you imagine the crowds, and all that money? We can't risk anyone finding a stray containment unit lying around, giving away our secrets."

"Did you hear that?" Vicki poked me and whispered in my ear. "He said 'real ghosts'. He is behind it."

I swallowed the lump in my throat. Vicki was right. Rex Rangler was a ghostnapper.

"I thought I heard someone." One of the guards took three steps towards us and peered down. I scrunched under the overhang as far as I could. Vicki held her breath. He seemed to stare right over us, and Vicki started to shake, her lips quivering.

The guard took a sniff. "Smells like gum."

Vicki's eyes bulged and with a giant swallow she swallowed her bubblegum.

"Never mind that," Rangler said. "Get this crate inside."

The guard turned away and walked back to the door next to Rangler.

Vicki let out a breath and rubbed her throat. "That was close. Let's listen and maybe he'll tell us how to get the ghosts out."

"That only happens in films," I said. "Real bad guys aren't dumb enough to tell you how to defeat them."

"Get this thing inside," Rangler said. "And be careful not to touch it. Once we empty it into the ectoplasmic projector, we'll be able to bring the ghosts out for display anytime we want." He rubbed his hands together with glee. "When the permanent containment unit is operating, they won't be able to escape. I'm glad we tested it at the old museum. It's a work of genius, if I do say so myself."

He wiggled his eyebrows, which were almost as big as his moustache. They looked like wings and he was ready for take-off.

Vicki grinned.

"Well, *sometimes* films are like real life," I said.

"Dan!"

Vicki and I both spun around at the sound of a bike skidding to a stop behind us.

"Dan, I've been looking for you. Want your drink?"

Luke hefted a huge drink over his head. Then he frowned at Vicki. "Didn't you leave?"

It only took Rangler and the guards a second to work out this boy with the monster-sized drinking cup wasn't talking to them. The toe of a blinking boot appeared over my head.

I sped off, but ran head-on into a security guard, flattening my nose on his plastic badge. A guard called Brick scooped me up by my arms.

"Let me go!" Vicki had made it a bit further than I had, but the other guard ran her down before she could round the building. Kicking her legs and flailing, she struggled as he carried her under an arm. The same guard dragged Luke with his other hand. He'd spilled his drink all over the car park.

"Watch it! I paid three pounds for that drink. You owe me."

Rex Rangler stared at me while Brick pinned my arms at my sides. My feet were half a metre off the ground.

"Do I know you?" He squinted and furrowed his brow.

"No."

"Wait, wait." He looked back and forth between me and Vicki. "You're that boy . . . those children, with all the questions about ghosts, aren't you? Come back to see for yourselves?"

Rangler waved at the guard holding Vicki and Luke to let them down. Luke stared at his drink-stained shirt, looking like he might try to suck it clean with his straw.

"You're just curious," Rangler said. "No crime in sneaking in without a ticket."

I let out a sigh, but I was still being squeezed by Brick.

"Well, there is a law, technically. It's called trespassing. But I suppose we can overlook that, this time."

Brick dropped me like a rock.

"Cool suit," Luke said.

"You have an eye for fine clothing, young man." Rangler admired his own outfit. The tiny LED lights flickered against the rhinestones outlining the dinosaurs. "Sorry for the mistake, but you can't be too careful. We've had a few people who couldn't wait until we opened to see what was inside. Ghostville promises to be a revolution in ghostly/paranormal entertainment, and there are unscrupulous people out there who'd pay lots of money to discover my secrets." He glanced sideways as if someone was listening.

I bit my lip. I couldn't let him know that I'd heard anything.

"We just wanted to see inside," Vicki said. "You know, dinosaurs."

Well done, Vicki. Maybe we could get out of here without giving up *our* secrets.

But there was still Luke. Luckily he didn't know what was going on, so of course he couldn't blow it.

"Dan," Luke said. "Did you tell him about those two ghosts at the museum, and ask for help finding your grandma and the other kidnapped ghosts?"

Rangler went stiff. First his moustache bolted out like it had springs. Then his eyebrow wings started flapping. He looked like one of those old biplanes.

"Kidnapped! What do you mean, kidnapped?"

"Er..." I said. "What?" I took a quick look at Luke like I didn't know what he was talking about. "Um . . . what?"

"Dan," Luke said. "You didn't forget about your grandma's ghost already, did you?"

Thanks, Luke.

Rangler grabbed my arm. His whole body shook. He seemed to be noticing for the first time that the crate was broken. "You appear to be the instigator here. What did you see? What two ghosts at the old museum?"

I grunted. "Nothing."

"Calm down," Luke said. "Tell him, Dan."

I leaned away from Rangler's moustache. It threatened to poke my eyes out if he got any closer.

"What two ghosts?" he asked again.

I kept quiet.

Rangler sniffed. "Perhaps I should call the police and see what they think about trespassing."

"I thought you said you'd overlook us not having tickets," I said.

"I lied."

"No." Vicki tried to pull her arm free. "I don't want to go to prison."

"Then tell me about those two ghosts," Rangler said. "What do you know?"

"Nothing," I said. "Let us go."

"Hey, you," Luke said.

Rangler turned with a snarl. Luke whipped his dino poo out of his pocket and splatted the ghostnapper right between the eyes. The goo slithered over his face, sticking to his wing-like eyebrows.

Rangler yelped and swiped at the blob. Tiny bits pulled loose, covered with hair. The goo attacked his face like zombie bubblegum. I kicked my guard in the knee, grabbed Vicki's hand and ran.

"Let's get out of here!"

Luke was ahead of me. Without a huge drink in his hand he moved pretty fast. We bolted past his bike, rounding the building and racing to the front car park where hundreds of people were still queuing to get inside the Dino Barn. In a few seconds we lost ourselves in the crowd, ducking down and pretending to be with all the other children waiting for tickets. Rangler stopped at the corner of the building. I imagine he didn't want to be seen chasing three children with poo on his face.

When we'd stopped running, I slapped Luke on the back. "Wow, good one. That dino poo really worked."

Luke frowned. "Those guards spilled my drink and now they have my dino poo. I should get a free ticket."

Vicki seemed happy with Luke. "I'll buy you one when we save Dan's grandma and Rangler's in prison."

Luke stared at her for a second. I think he was still wondering why I was spending time with Vicki, or maybe imagining what she'd look like with goo stuck to her face. He shrugged. "Whatever."

Luke had to leave his bike behind, so he sat on my handlebars on the way home. My bike creaked and groaned under the extra weight and I couldn't see around him. Luckily I only nicked two trees and a parked car. No real damage. To me anyway.

When we were out of sight of the Dino Barn, Vicki pulled up next to me. "Rangler knows about Adams and Mr Greensocks. We should go back and warn them before he shows up."

I nodded. I didn't want Rangler to snatch anyone else. And maybe Adams could give us some clues about how to get Grandma out of that black hole.

"So is she going to hang around with us all the time now?" Luke asked as I weaved and wobbled down the street while checking over my shoulder for any pursuit. Vicki pulled ahead and I hoped she couldn't hear us.

"Uh, yeah, I suppose so. She's not that bad. I'd never have found my grandma without her. So she's okay. But don't tell her that, it's a secret."

"That's a secret I can keep." Luke scowled.

Vicki dropped back next to us and leaned over towards me. "I have secret." She whispered so Luke couldn't hear. "I think you're okay, too."

CHAPTER FOURTEEN

BEING A GHOST

After we'd escaped from Rex Rangler and his guards, Luke, Vicki and I raced home to come up with a new plan. Halfway back Vicki's phone buzzed.

"But Mum," Vicki said. "I told you I was with a friend. His name's Dan . . . No, his mum knows me . . . okay." She clicked off her phone. "I have to go home. Sorry. I'll convince my mum by tomorrow that you're nice. Then I can help you again."

"Don't bother," Luke said.

I elbowed him and nodded at Vicki. "Okay. Make sure you do."

Vicki grinned. "I will." After a few more streets, she turned off for her house.

"Finally," Luke said over his shoulder as Vicki rode away. "We don't need her. We can find your grandma by ourselves."

"Why don't you want her to come?"

Luke rolled his eyes. "Just because."

"Because why? I told you she was okay. I wish you'd stop teasing her."

"Stop teasing her?" Luke elbowed me. "That's what we do. She's not one of us. We're a team. We don't need anyone else."

Luke was right; we did everything as a team, especially get into trouble. We stuck up for each other. When Grandma died he didn't even mind when I sat in his bedroom without talking and didn't want to play video games. It was always me and Luke and no one else. But Vicki was different. I didn't know why.

I slapped him on the back. "Just stop teasing her, okay?"

"Whatever," Luke said, looking away. We rode the rest of the way home in silence.

* * *

Dad took Mum and me out for pizza and then ice cream that night. Dad seemed a lot happier than I'd seen him in forever.

"Ham and pineapple, Dan?" Dad asked. "Your favourite, right?"

"Yeah. No rice."

The pizza was really good and I ate like a pig. Halfway through my seventh slice, my stomach stabbed at me and I started feeling guilty. I thought back to when Grandma used to come over on pizza night. Once she told me how she'd met Grandpa over a pizza. She stuck pepperoni to her nose. "This was how I got Grandpa to notice me on our first date," she'd said, doing a dance. Grandma loved pizza.

I wondered if Vicki liked pizza.

Mum must have noticed me stop in the middle of my slice. "Dan, are you okay? Getting full?"

"No. Just needed to breathe." I wolfed down the rest of the slice so fast I got sauce burn. I didn't want Mum or Dad asking me how I felt or trying to stick a torch in my mouth. And the faster I ate, the easier it was to keep both Grandma and Vicki out of my thoughts. I ordered the extra-huge chocolate fudge caramel sundae with nuts to ease my pain.

"Slow down," Mum said. "You must be feeling better. At least until you notice how much you've eaten."

Dad burped. "Can't have too much of a good thing."

Mum rolled her eyes and Dad winked at me. He knew she disliked his deep, resonant burps, but they always made me laugh. He hadn't burped at the table in months. I missed them.

I opened my mouth to let out the blast of the century.

"Don't you dare, mister," Mum said, laughing. "That's what I get for having two boys." She shook her head, but I could see her huge smile. I really liked hearing her laugh again.

Mum was right though. I couldn't sleep that night because my stomach felt like I'd swallowed a box of boulders. I laid awake thinking of those crazy stairs and Grandma trapped in some weird alternate-dimension bowling ball. The more I thought about that, the more my gut ached. What if I couldn't get her out? What if I couldn't stop Rangler and he succeeded in putting her into his amusement park? I was so happy to see her again. What if the next time she was a display, like those robot dinosaurs? I tapped out a text, but there was no answer. I hid under my pillow until the sun rose, then I got up before Dad left for work.

"Where are you off to so early? Looking for ghosts again?" he asked me.

I shrugged and tried not to look scared. I didn't know how to tell him that his boss was a ghostnapper. "Just meeting Luke."

Dad furrowed his brow and stared at me for a moment. What had he noticed? I smiled.

"You look like you swallowed an insect."

"Just a pizza."

"Yeah, it didn't sit too well with me either." He grinned and rubbed his stomach. "I suppose we need to wean ourselves off the rice more slowly. Well, I'm going to work. Hopefully I won't always have to go on weekends. When I get some time we'll do something fun. I'll take you to Ghostville when it opens. I'm sure I'll get an employee discount. Doesn't that sound good?"

I choked up and had to turn away to hide my eyes. Thinking about walking into Ghostville with Mum and Dad and seeing Grandma on display like a circus freak left me short of breath. Would they even notice it was her? Would anyone suspect that Rangler had enslaved real ghosts? I swallowed my tears. "Yeah. Great. Can't wait."

Dad wrapped his arm around my shoulder. "I can't tell you how excited I am about this job. I know it's been hard for you, too. First losing your grandma, then having to eat rice all the time. But things really will be better from now on." He put his finger under my chin and tilted my head up to look at him. "Sorry if I've been a bit of a drudge lately. I'll make it up to you."

"That's okay. I understand."

"You know you can talk to me about anything, right?"

"Yeah. I know." I almost told him everything right then, but it would have spoiled his new job.

"Have a great day, Dan."

"You too, Dad."

After Dad drove off in his Rangler Enterprises lorry I met Vicki at the corner. She'd obviously convinced her mum that I was safe. Luke wasn't there. He'd always been there before.

"Hi, Vicki." I gave her a little wave.

"Hi, Dan." She smiled back, wiggling her fingers at me.

I didn't know why, but my hand reached up on its own and tried to straighten my hair. Maybe *I was haunted*.

My mouth went off on its own, too. "Um . . . do you like pizza?"

"Yeah. I love pizza."

"Me too," I said.

Vicki grinned. "Ready to go?"

I looked around to see if Luke would show. The street was empty. It was just me and Vicki. "I suppose so."

I was climbing on my bike when I heard a shout from across the street. "Dan, what's wrong with you? Were you going without me?"

I waited for Luke to join us. "I didn't think you'd show up." I wanted him to come, but I was still mad.

Luke grunted and looked sideways at Vicki. "No, I'm coming. You need someone who knows what they're doing."

"No teasing," I said.

"Whatever."

We took off for the old museum to warn our ghost friends that Rangler knew about them. I tried to ride next to Vicki, but Luke kept cutting in between. He had borrowed his little sister Teko's bike and whacked his knees on the handlebars.

"At least she took off the training wheels." I laughed as Luke struggled to keep riding straight. "That's a cute basket, though, and I really love those frilly things on the handles. You look totally fast."

"Shut up!"

It was Sunday and without much traffic we made it to the museum pretty fast. We ditched our bikes by the kerb. The old building was still abandoned, no cars in the car park and not a sign of anyone. I creaked open the doors and we slipped in.

"Mr Adams?" Vicki called out. "Mr Greensocks? Are you there?"

The place was dark except for the always flickering red neon *Egress* sign.

"Oh, cool," Luke said. "Egress. I saw one in a film. It's some kind of giant people-eating bird with a sharp beak and octopus arms. It had rocket-powered farts, too." He shot off, following the arrow and in a second disappeared around the corner.

Rocket-powered farts? I wished.

"Should we tell him?" Vicki asked.

"He'll be back."

Running up to the first floor, I searched for any signs of the ghosts. I checked my ecto-meter. It was flat-lined. Were we too late?

"Adams! Where are you?"

No answer.

"Where could they be?" Vicki chomped on a new piece of gum. She chewed harder when she was nervous. She tried to blow a bubble again, and this time the wad landed on my foot. I didn't even mind.

"Please pick that up and throw it away," a voice behind me said. "No gum allowed in the cinema."

I whipped around to find Mr Greensocks's familiar paleness floating half a metre off the ground. He was pointing at my shoe.

"Oh good. We were looking for you. We found where the ghosts are, but we don't know how to get them out. I thought you might know. Oh, and Rangler's coming, so we have to hide you, too. Where's Adams?"

Mr Greensocks stared at me, shaking his head and pointing at my foot.

"Did you hear me? Rangler's coming."

"The gum, if you please," Mr Greensocks said. "In the bin."

He was pretty fussy about stepping in something for a man whose feet didn't touch the ground. I leaned over to grab the gum and knocked heads with Vicki. "I've got it."

"Thanks."

Her fingers touched mine just as I picked up the gum. My hand tingled. I got confused for a second and stuffed the gum in my pocket. It squished into my pocket money. Vicki giggled.

Satisfied that I wasn't a litterbug, the ghost of the old cinema owner lifted up towards the rafters like a puff of smoke. He misted right through the ceiling and vanished.

"I wish I could do that," I said. "Except without the having to be dead first thing."

Vicki smiled and nodded. "You never told me about your grandma. Is she okay?"

"Well, she didn't like being held prisoner, and inside

that ball was really weird. It was all stairs leading nowhere, just back into each other. She really wanted to get out."

"What's it like being dead?"

My chest went cold. Whenever I thought about Grandma being dead I felt like I was stuck in a freezer. But it seemed different now. She wasn't just someone I used to know and love. Yes, she was trapped in that weird every-dimensional place, but I didn't think of her as dead anymore, just a bit different. Kind of hazy and transparent, but still Grandma.

I shrugged. "I'm not sure. She didn't talk about it."

"Where will the ghosts go when we free them?" Vicki asked. "All those old houses have been torn down." She looked up at the ceiling. Greensocks hadn't come back. "Maybe they'll just move on."

"Move on?" The cold came back. "What do you mean? I told my grandma she could live with us at my house. I'm sure my mum and dad won't mind."

"Are you sure?" Vicki asked. "I think most ghosts move on after a while. That's why they're so hard to find. Their spirits don't stay here for very long after they die."

My gut dropped. I'd just found Grandma again. I didn't want to lose her a second time.

"I don't think so." I shook my head. "She'll want to stay with me."

Wouldn't she?

Vicki stared at me for a moment, not saying anything. She nodded. "Yeah, she probably will." Then she turned away. I saw a small tear run down her cheek. Her voice cracked a bit as she asked, "Did you . . . did you see anyone else in there?"

"Yeah. There were a load of ghosts. Some weird pink woman with a freaky dog, and lots of others. They were kind of creepy at first. But I got used to it."

"Was there a man there, in . . . in a uniform? Like the army?" Her eyes got really big and wet.

I scratched my head, trying to remember. Besides the pink woman and Grandma, everyone else was a blur. "No, I didn't see anyone from the army. Why?"

"I just thought . . . oh, no reason. Just wondering."

There was something Vicki wasn't telling me. Who was she looking for?

"Are you sure?" I asked.

She looked at the ground and started to mumble, sniffing and wiping at her eyes, "Well, I . . ."

Just then I heard a whoop from the ground floor. We ran downstairs and saw Adams near the ceiling, drifting down like a cloud, waving his hat around his head. "You're back! And you found that prison. Let's go and catch a ghostnapper!"

CHAPTER FIFTEEN

PRISON BREAK

Vicki and I had found Adams before Rangler got to him. Luke was outside. He'd fallen for the old egress trick. I raced towards the door, stopping just before I opened it. I glanced back at Adams.

"You'll get turned into spaghetti," I said.

Adams grinned. "Been doing some investigating. I think I've found out how it works."

Just then the door flew open.

"Dan," Luke said, stumbling his way back inside. "There's no egress, just the exit."

A tornado blew up around my feet and Luke's hair stood on end. Adams swirled like he'd been flushed down a toilet. I covered my eyes from the dust, and Adams and Mr Greensocks slowly whipped into noodles.

"Close it!" I pointed at Luke, shouting. He slammed the door and the wind stopped. The two ghosts regained their normal shapes.

Luke grabbed my shoulder and spun me around. "Are those the ghosts? They're so amazing!"

I nodded. "The one in the battered old jacket is Richard Adams, the local railway pioneer."

"No way. I've heard that name before."

"We go to school at Richard Adams Secondary School."

A light flashed on in Luke's eyes. "That's him? That's Richard Adams?"

"I know. Cool, eh?"

Adams floated beside us, a shadow under a hat. He had an old musket slung over one shoulder and a jagged, ghostly knife big enough to be a sword strapped to his hip. He tipped his hat to Luke. "Nice to meet you."

"That's so cool," Luke said.

"I thought you had the egress worked out." I said to Adams.

He frowned. "Let me check one more thing." Adams wafted back up towards the ceiling, right into the egress sign.

I looked around for Vicki. She was trailing behind with her hands in her pockets, staring at the floor. I walked back over to her. There were streaks running down her face. She caught me staring and wiped her nose.

"You okay?"

"The soldier," she said. "He's my dad. I was hoping maybe he did come home from the war after all. I wanted to say goodbye."

Vicki's dad was dead? I never knew that. I thought when she said he wasn't around that her parents were divorced. She hadn't told anyone at school, even on Veterans Day when Mr Brakenbush talked about soldiers dying in the war. But she had mentioned visiting a cemetery and that her mum didn't like ghosts because she didn't want to be reminded of something. I suppose that explains why Vicki was so interested in finding ghosts with me and had asked all those questions about Grandma dying, and maybe even why she was a bit weird. I'd be weird too if my dad went off to war and never came home. I'd been really weird after Grandma died. It's funny how people are different once you know something about them.

Sometimes they don't even seem weird anymore.

"Sorry," I said.

Vicki cracked a thin smile. "Thanks." She reached out and touched my hand for a second. I grabbed a finger. This time the tingling felt warm, too.

Adams let out another whoop. I looked up and saw him twirling around the flashing sign. Drifting in and out from between the letters he popped his head through the hole in the G and winked. "I was right. This is what's been keeping us here."

"But that's just an exit sign," I said. "It's not an exit."

"Open the door."

"But . . ."

"Just open it, and look up here."

I nodded at Luke and he pulled the door open.

I hadn't noticed before, but the sign brightened and glowed even more strongly, like glowing coals when you blow on them. And of course the ghosts got blenderized.

"That's enough!" I shouted above the wind. Luke slammed the door.

"Looks like some kind of force field that turns on when you open the door," I said. "That must be how that ghost prison works, too."

"That's more than I know," Adams said. "But there's only one solution – break it!"

"Whoo hoo! I can do that." Luke instantly ran to an open broom cupboard. Piece after piece of junk flew out and crashed at my feet. "Got it!" Luke jumped out waving an old dented bucket and a broken mop handle.

"Here, Dan." He handed me the bucket. "You try knocking it down with this, and I'll use the spear."

Vicki cleared her throat. "Is there something *I* can throw?"

"I don't know," Luke said. "Can *girls* throw?"

"Shut up, Luke." I handed Vicki the bucket. "Here, try this." I leaned over and whispered, "Your dad might be there. I didn't really look too closely. I just wanted to find my grandma."

"That's okay," she said. "I'm sure he isn't. I'm used to it now."

Luke glared at me, shaking his head. "Dan, I don't even know you. I can't believe you've really got a girlfriend."

What was he talking about? Vicki was just my friend.

"Shut up and throw your spear. We have to get out of here. Hurry!"

Luke turned around and gripped his weapon, gritting his teeth. "Whatever."

He reached back and just like we always practised against the side of the garage with any heavy sticks we could find, he launched it at the sign. And just like always the mop handle sailed right by, missing the glass tubes by a foot.

"Let me try again." Luke dashed over to retrieve the stick. "I'll get it this time."

But before he could even reach his spear I saw the bucket arch out of Vicki's hand, tumble overhead and smash straight into the E of egress. Red sparks zinged in a giant rainbow as tiny glass pieces rained down on us.

"That's for your grandma."

I snatched up the fallen bucket and hurled it again as Luke ducked away from the shards of glass. This time the missile brought down the rest of the sign in a big spray. Luke plucked the glass out of his hair.

"That's for your dad."

"Well done, you two," Adams said. "Looks like we've

got a man and a woman of action. Shall we go to the rescue?"

I reached for the door and slowly pulled it open. There was no wind, no sucking, no swirling, no flushing.

One prison break down, one to go.

CHAPTER SIXTEEN

ON THE RUN

Now that Vicki and I had broken the egress sign that held Adams and Mr Greensocks hostage, there was nothing to keep us from leaving the old museum where Rangler had been testing his ghost prison. We all dashed out of the door, including the two ghosts who floated right beside us.

"So who is this villain holding my friends, and your dear grandmother?" Adams asked. "I can't wait to get my hands on him."

"His name's Rex Rangler," Vicki said.

"Rangler, huh? Sounds like a horse thief. We used to hang horse thieves." He reached around his throat and pretended to pull, making his eyes bulge and his tongue stick out.

"We found a weird black hole at the Dino Barn with the ghosts inside it," I said. "I stuck my head in and talked to my grandma."

Adams's jaw dropped. "Stuck your head in, you say?

Well, good for you. You're far braver than I. No wonder your grandmother trusts you. I'm a bit embarrassed to be hiding. Is everyone all right?"

I nodded. "They're all okay, but Rangler caught us. He wants to have real ghosts for a haunted museum. He's coming here to get you."

"Then let's get going. We can hang him later."

The screech of tyres interrupted us. A van whizzed into the car park and squealed to a stop. Led by Brick, three of Rangler's security guards jumped out. Brick carried a long hose connected to what looked like the black hole that held Grandma.

"Whoa there." Adams hovered over my head to get a better look. "I've seen that thing before. I'd just as soon not get too close."

"Then we better run."

With Adams flying next to my right ear, we headed behind the building to the back gate. I checked over my shoulder for the cinema owner. He was still behind us, staring like a deer caught in headlights.

Brick pointed his ghost hose at Mr Greensocks. His eyes bulged and then his ears wiggled and flopped and what little hair he had jetted out over his face. In another second his arms and legs shot straight forward and he was sucked into the hose. It was a ghost vacuum cleaner.

"They got him!" Vicki screamed, turning around. "We have to go back."

"We can't help him now." Adams waved us on. "Keep moving."

I'm a pretty fast runner, and Luke isn't too bad either. I was afraid we might lose Vicki, so I slowed down, but she blew right past me. She's a much better runner than bubblegum-bubble blower.

"Where are we going?" Luke leaned on his knees and panted after we'd made it out of the car park.

I looked at Vicki. "Back to the Dino Barn to free my grandma," I said. "That's what we came for."

"They'll be waiting for us," Luke said.

"It's the only thing we can do," Vicki said. "There isn't anyone left to ask for help. We have to do it ourselves."

The van rumbled around the corner. I saw Brick at the wheel, grinning behind his sunglasses. He loved his job too much.

"Down that alley," I said, pointing. It looked narrow and crowded with rubbish bins. Luke dashed in first and I ducked in behind Vicki. Adams flew over my head. The van spun its tyres and screeched after us.

I pushed over a bin to block the entrance, but the van didn't even slow down. Brick crashed right through in a spray of wet paper and rotten food. Up ahead a chain-link fence blocked the end of the passage.

"Oh, no." Vicki rattled the fence. "We're trapped."

I looked around for another way out, but there were no doors and no way around the fence. The van slowed to a crawl and inched its way towards us.

"There's no egress." I liked saying egress.

"Yeah, we definitely could use some exploding farts at the moment," Luke said.

"What?"

"It would cut right through the fence."

"Oh, good idea."

Adams wafted down from over my head. He straightened his hat, fluffed his beard, whipped his musket off his shoulder and attached his wicked knife to the barrel as a bayonet. He pointed it towards the van. "It's about time I lived up to my reputation as a fighter." He pulled back the hammer on his gun. "No more running or hiding while my friends suffer. You lot climb over that fence while I hold the guards off. I'll give you enough time to get away and then follow after you."

"Wait. Will that gun work?" I asked. "I know my grandma's phone sends texts, but ghosts can't touch anyone."

Adams grinned. "Let's find out." Then he let out a wild screeching whoop and zoomed off down the alley. A roar and a flash and a puff of smoke erupted from his rifle.

Brick and the other guards, who'd climbed out of the van by now, flinched and dived back behind the opened doors for cover while Adams reloaded.

Ghost guns did work.

"That'll teach you to mess with the man who set up the railway in this town! Now go on! Run!"

I jumped up onto the fence, gripping the rough metal and wedging my feet into the small diamond-shaped openings. It was a tight fit, but I got enough of a foothold to start climbing. Luke was already near the top and Vicki raced up right behind me. Then I heard Brick shout, "Wait a minute. He's a ghost. He can't shoot us."

Ghost guns don't work.

In another second Brick dived back into the van and grabbed his ghost vacuum. "You won't get away this time." He aimed the hose at Adams. My ghost friend was still ramming another bullet down the barrel of his gun when he looked up in amazement. First his hat whipped off his head, and then the musket flew out of his hand. In a blinding swirl Adams twisted and spun.

"Run!" he said one last time. Then he was sucked away.

I stopped at the top of the fence, one leg hanging over. Without Adams, I had no idea how to free Grandma.

"Hurry, Dan." Luke dropped down the other side of the fence and landed on the pavement.

"But we need him."

"They'll get you, too." I'd never seen Luke this careful about me before.

Vicki sat on the top of the fence with me. She reached out and gave me a small shove. My feet slipped but I managed to grab hold with one hand. Vicki had pushed me to my death, again, just like at the lift at the old museum.

"Hey. Watch it."

"Sorry. But you have to save your grandma." Then she turned and jumped.

"What are you doing? They'll get you. I need you."

"You can do this, Dan. I have to see for myself if my dad is in there."

Before I could move Vicki balled her fists and dashed straight at the still-sucking ghost-vacuum. I hoped that it wouldn't work on a real person, but in the blink of an eye Vicki's feet whipped off the ground and she twirled and stretched, her arms flailing. In another second she'd vanished.

Luke grabbed my arm and pulled me down the next street. We ran until we couldn't breathe anymore. We'd lost Brick and the other guards.

And Vicki.

I hoped she would find her dad.

CHAPTER SEVENTEEN

G-G-GIRLFRIEND

Vicki was gone, sucked into the ghost vacuum by Brick, Rangler's number-one thug. Luke and I ran. We were a dozen streets away when I spotted the Rangler Enterprises van again. I pulled Luke down behind a parked car, interrupting his after-kidnapping snack.

"That was my last chocolate bar." He stared at it floating in the gutter. I think he was close to tears.

I pointed at the van, but Brick drove right by without looking. I realized he had what he wanted. He'd captured Adams and Vicki, and I had no way of getting them back. My stomach ached and I couldn't breathe. I was just getting to know her.

I sat down on the kerb and felt something sticky. Chocolate and nuts, just what I needed. I didn't even bother wiping it off my bum. Vicki had come up with all the ideas. I just stuck my head into things. Or sat on them.

"I'm sorry, Vicki," I said to myself. "Please help her, Grandma."

Luke kicked my foot. "You coming? We have to get to the Dino Barn and rescue your grandma."

I grunted and stared at my feet. I couldn't rescue anybody. I'd messed up everything. I was much better at getting people captured.

"Come on." Luke gave me a shove. "Let's move."

"Since when are you so helpful?" I glared at him.

Luke frowned and stared back at me. "Since always. We're a team, remember?"

"A team! Vicki was the only one I could count on. You were too busy being an idiot."

"Me? You're the one who ran off with a girl."

"Ran off? What are you talking about?"

Luke rolled his eyes and then glared at me. "You left me so you could spend time with her. That's not cool."

"I asked you to come. Why did you have to be such an idiot?"

"Is that why you're spending time with her, because you think I'm stupid and she's clever?"

I stared at Luke. What was wrong with him? "No, but Vicki is cool too. I can have more than one friend."

Luke sighed and shook his head. "I . . . You're my only friend."

I gaped at Luke. He'd never told me how he felt about anything before, except when I kicked him in the shins, and he told me with a punch. I suppose I had never said how I felt either. "You're still my best friend. But Vicki is my friend, too." I looked away. "Was my friend. She's gone, and it's my fault."

Luke shook his head. "I'm still not sure why you care, but Vicki's going to be fine. Weren't you inside that thing? You got out."

"Only because Vicki was clever enough to save me."

"You're the clever one. You always come up with good ideas. Think of one now. Your grandma needs you. And so does Vicki. I don't like her, but you do, for some reason. Let's go and rescue her. She already saved you."

I sat and stared, picking at the chocolate on my trousers. Luke was right. Vicki would do it for me.

But how?

Luke held out his hand to help me up. "Mates?" he asked.

"Mates."

Just then a van screeched to a halt in front of us. On the door it said *Rangler Enterprises.*

"Dan, run!" Luke jerked my arm and took off up the street. The tug pulled me off balance and I fell to the pavement. I looked up expecting to see Brick or another of Rangler's men with that vacuum. The window on the door lowered.

"You okay, Dan?" My dad stuck his head out of the window. I'd forgotten that he was working for Rangler. "Where's Luke off to? Run out of chocolate?"

"Something like that."

Luke must have seen my dad, because he showed up a few seconds later, panting. "Too much running. Need food."

I thought it was about time I told Dad what was going on. Maybe he could work out what to do.

"Um, Dad . . ." I got into the van while Luke shoved me and wiped his hands on my back. "There's something about this man you work for that you should know . . ."

I told Dad everything, even about Vicki nearly pushing me over the fence. He stared, his eyes gaping open. He didn't say anything, just shook his head, even after I had finished.

"You believe me, don't you? It's all true, everything. I swear."

"It's true." Luke took a bite and licked his fingers. He'd magically found a back-up snack. "I didn't believe it either, at least the girlfriend part, 'cause that's just crazy. But it's all true."

"I never said anything about a girlfriend."

"Dan, face it, you've got a girlfriend." He poked me in the ribs. "A g-i-r-l-f-r-ahhh . . . end."

I glanced at Dad. I hoped he wasn't listening to this part. "No, Vicki's my friend, and she's a girl, but that's not the same thing."

"I know what I'm talking about," Luke said. "You have a girlfriend. A g-i-r— "

"I know how to spell it."

"That's 'cause you have one."

I was just about to punch him when Dad finally spoke up. "So that's what's been bothering you. Girlfriends are nice." He nodded and grinned. "No reason to be ashamed about that, even when they almost kill you. That's part of the deal. They're not really your girlfriend until they almost kill you."

"Do you believe me? About the ghosts, I mean?"

"It's crazy like Luke said, but I don't think you'd make up something like that, even with the chocolate fiend's help, especially not girlfriends. That's going too far." He ruffled my hair.

"What about your job? I don't want you to lose it."

Dad put his arm around me and squeezed. "Dan, I know I said I was excited, but that's because I knew I'd be able to do more for you and your mum now. A job is just what I do, it's not who I am. Who I am is a man who raised a son who's so brave and cares so much about his grandma and his girlfriend that he's willing to stick his head into another dimension to save them. That's worth more than any job in the world." He winked. "I'm really proud of you. Let's go and rescue your grandma, and Vicki."

"See?" Luke said, poking me in the ribs. "Girlfriend."

"Shut up!"

Dad started up the engine. "We can eat rice

casserole for a while longer. I'm used to it, and that pizza nearly did me in. Who wants to work for a criminal anyway?"

"Thanks, Dad."

We raced off to Ghostville. Now I just had to work out what to do when we got there.

CHAPTER EIGHTEEN

PULL THE PLUG

Dad flew through town, beeping and weaving in and out of traffic on the way to the Dino Barn / Ghostville. Luke spilled out a thousand ideas for defeating Rangler.

"We don't have any ray guns." I checked my pockets to make sure. "Or teleporters. And those rocket-powered farts aren't real."

"Dan, you lie. I'm sure about the farts. That egress thing was really stinky."

"No time machines either," Dad said. "But that is a good idea to go back to fix things before they happen. Then I wouldn't have to miss my lunch break."

Normally I can listen to Luke's schemes all day long, and still spend the evening cleaning up and explaining why I shouldn't be grounded. But time was running out. We had to free Grandma and Vicki before Rangler got his permanent ghost prison up and running.

"They've been putting in some heavy-duty power lines," Dad said. "And big back-up generators. Looks like they want whatever they're powering to survive a nuclear war."

"I saw those yesterday," I said. "Rangler said that once he put the ghosts in the display they can never escape. We have to get there before he turns all that stuff on. When are they supposed to finish with the power lines?"

Dad frowned. "Um, well, I think it was today. The Dino Barn is closed for the work. We better hurry."

My stomach turned. The one at the old museum had kept Adams trapped without the huge power lines. This new one was different. Rangler had said he could control the ghosts at Ghostville, and Adams had still been free to move around inside the museum. Maybe that's what the extra power was for: strings to make the puppets dance. We didn't have much time.

Dad accelerated so quickly that I was pushed against the seat. Luke's chocolate bar shot out of the window as we flew through traffic like a rocket-powered fart.

When we pulled up behind the Dino Barn, Dad let Luke and me out. I saw Brick's van parked by the loading dock. A brand new transformer hummed and buzzed in the car park.

"We're too late."

Dad shook his head. "No way. You two get inside where it's safe. I'll take care of the power. Hopefully the back-up isn't running yet."

I stood back and stared at Dad while he pulled a thick cable out of the winch in his lorry and wrapped it around the transformer. He connected it back to the other end of the cable and climbed back in. "Good thing they trust me with a lorry. Now get going. Once I've pulled the plug you won't have long. The back-up generators may be close to going online. Oh, and don't touch anything electrical or metal, just in case."

"Just in case of what?" Luke asked.

"ZZZZZZZZZZZZZZZ."

"Ouch."

I pulled my ecto-meter out and turned it on. I crossed my fingers, hoping we were close enough for Grandma to get my text.

C-o-m-i-n-g, I typed.

"Dan," Dad said, leaning out of the window. "I'll follow you in after I pull this thing loose. Don't try to take on Rangler by yourself. He's too dangerous."

I nodded and then Luke and I ran for the loading dock.

"I kind of wanted to stay and see the transformer explode," Luke said after we'd crept up to the back door. "That'd be cool. BOOM! But you'd never get anywhere without my help."

I glared at him. He laughed and punched me, but this time he was right. I was glad to have my best friend helping me again.

Luckily the door was open and no alarms went off. Brick must have forgotten to lock up.

When I'd been inside the Dino Barn the first time, I'd noticed that there was a whole other huge section to the building that wasn't being used for the dinosaur exhibits. That had to be where Rangler was setting up the haunted house. Waving Luke on, I rushed inside. We ran past boxes and crates marked "dino parts", "ghost sheets" and "flashing suits". Rangler needed back-ups for everything.

We were lucky that the museum was closed. The last two days had been a sneak peek. Today there were no crowds, and no one seemed to be working either. Maybe Rangler wanted to keep his ghosts a secret until the last moment. When we reached the exhibit floor, we crept behind a Tyrannosaurus robot to scout out the scene.

"Wow, these robots are so cool." Luke stared up at the mechanical jaws hanging over our heads. "I wonder if you can ride them. That would be fantastic."

I shrugged. I didn't have time to think about any new amusement park rides. Although a Tyrannosaurus ride would be cool.

"Try to find that black ball before the power goes out," I said. "Once it's dark, we won't be able to see it and we'll have to act fast before the power comes back on."

"Aren't we waiting for your dad?"

"If there's time."

I crossed my fingers. How long could Vicki survive in that ball? Ghosts could get by without food and water, and a toilet, but Vicki needed all of those. I wished we'd had more time and a better plan.

"I bet you could crawl up inside that dinosaur and get to the controls," Luke said. "There's a little hatch right here." He pointed at a small door on the belly.

"We don't have time. We need to find that ball."

"I never saw the ball before. What does it look like?"

"Yes you did. That's what they used to suck up Vicki."

"What?"

"It's a small black ball." I held out my hands to bowling ball size. "Black, you know, and a ball. Black ball."

"Gotcha. Black ball. Not too big."

"Don't touch it, though. You might end up inside with Vicki."

"No problem there," he said. "So where is it? I don't see anything except dinosaurs."

He was right. We weren't going to find ghosts in the Dino Barn. Looking down at the far end of the hall I spotted a huge arched doorway with another box office next to it. It looked like another entrance, but what hung above made me doubly sure: a brand new *This Way to the Egress* sign.

The fake exit light wasn't lit yet.

"In there." I grabbed Luke's sleeve. "We've got to get the ghosts out before that sign comes on."

"Why don't we just smash it like the other one?"

"Hey, yeah," I said. "Good idea. Let's bust it up."

Luke was way ahead of me. Sprinting across the hall straight towards a collection of petrified dino poos, he snatched up a handful and headed for the sign. Based on his aim, I was pretty sure we'd be there all day.

Luke reared back and chucked his first fossil up at the sign. It was a miracle. It crashed right into the big *E*. But there were no flashes or fireworks or rain of glass, just a dull clunk. The rock bounced off, fell back and hit Luke in the shoulder.

"Ouch! What's going on?"

"I don't think it's glass." These lights looked harder than concrete. "Rangler made it unbreakable this time."

"Don't worry," Luke said. "Dino poo can do anything."

Gripping his load tightly, he tossed another chunk of poo.

Clunk.

Nothing.

Just then a huge crashing sound came from outside. All the lights flickered and then blinked out. *Dad*.

"Hey, it did work," Luke said, throwing his last poo anyway. "Just a bit slow."

"Well done, Dad!" I pumped my fist. Then I heard a

whoosh and a slam. The doors around the hall clanged shut and locked in one gigantic bang. Cutting the power must have activated some emergency security system, leaving Dad stuck outside – and Luke and me trapped inside. My whole body went cold. We were on our own.

CHAPTER NINETEEN

HALL OF GHOSTS

I tugged at one of the Dino Barn doors. Luke pulled on another. They were stuck. Every entrance had smashed closed when Dad destroyed the transformer and cut the power supply, trapping Luke and me inside and Dad on the outside. I took a deep breath and told myself it would be okay. I could do this; Luke was with me. But the nagging thought of Vicki turning into a ghost made me shiver.

"Can't wait for my dad," I said, shaking off the creepy feeling in my arms and legs. Then I typed, "I'm coming, Grandma," into my ecto-meter. I waved the meter around to get better reception. There was no answer. I needed to get closer.

Luckily there were no real doors between the dino hall and the ghost room, just some turnstiles. I pushed through the nearest one but forgot to warn Luke.

WHAM!

"Ouch! That hurts. I need those parts," he whimpered.

Luke must have been getting used to talking about his feelings.

"Sssssh!"

Luke's whining about his broken parts echoed through the hall. What looked like three or four torches popped on in the darkness.

"Get down," I said. "They'll see us."

"I can't bend over. I'll never walk again."

Luke stood his ground, sticking out like a beacon of pain shining on our covert operation. The lights spun around and lit him up like a bull's-eye.

My eyes hadn't adjusted to the dark yet and all I could see were bright spots. I rubbed them, and when I looked back I spotted four men standing around something still too black to make out. One of the men had a giant moustache, while another held a ghost vacuum. Rangler and Brick.

"Get them!" Rangler waved his hands and his torch beam whipped around the room like a firefly in a tornado. "And see about the power!"

Brick dropped the vacuum and shot off after us along with the other two guards.

I spun around, looking for a place to hide. This time *I* cracked into the turnstile.

I fell into Luke and tried to grab his arm to keep from falling over.

The jolt cured his injury. "I'm off!" He raced back into the dino hall. I flopped on the floor like a fish on the beach.

Brick leaped over me and the other two guards followed right behind him, ignoring me.

Rex Rangler aimed his torch at my face and reached into his pocket. I waited for him to pull out a stun gun, or maybe to suck me into his ghost prison. But in a second his suit flashed on. Strings of lights lit up the room. This suit had ghost figures on it.

"That's better." He squinted at me, his gargantuan eyebrow wings flaring. "You again. Who are you, anyway?"

"Dan Newton."

Tilting his head back, Rangler scratched his chin. "Newton, Newton, sounds familiar. Didn't I just hire a Newton? You aren't related, are you?"

"That's my dad, and he just shut off your power." I

wondered if I should be telling him this, but I felt like I was in a film, taunting my nemesis.

"The payroll needs trimming anyway."

I should have kept my mouth shut.

Rangler wiggled his forehead and his eyebrows danced up and down like hairy worms. "Well, now that you've helped me sort out my human resources problem, suppose you tell me why you keep getting in my way."

It was too late to save Dad's job, so I spilled the whole story. "I'm here to rescue my grandma and my friend and put an end to your evil ghostnapping plans."

Rangler's eyes flashed. "There's that awful word again, ghostnapping. If it really is a word, which it's not. Very commendable, however, your devotion to your grandmother. She's not here."

"Yes, she is. I saw her." I stood up and pointed at the black ball lying at Rangler's feet. "She's in there, with all the other ghosts you captured. And she wants out."

Rangler turned sideways and gave the ball a kick. His foot thudded against it and he cried, "Ouch!" It barely skittered across the floor. "Impossible. It's just a ball," he said, rubbing his foot.

"I was in it. I saw everything."

Rangler put his foot down and squinted at me. "So you think that having a haunted house is bad for some reason."

"No, I think kidnapping ghosts is bad."

He walked straight at me, pointing his finger in my face. "Don't you like fun? Ghosts are fun, you know. Scary fun."

"Ghosts are people." I pushed his finger away. "And you can't just put them in prison and use them for a show. That's illegal . . . and wrong."

Laughing, Rangler grabbed my hand and held it. "So you know the law too? Well, Mr Newton, show me where it's illegal to use ghosts for an amusement park. In fact, show me any law that even mentions ghosts." He dropped my hand and waited for a second, staring at me. "No? I thought not. Ghosts have no rights. They're dead."

"So? They're still people."

"Ridiculous. Ghosts are not people anymore. They're ectoplasmic remnants without any soul. If you watched my TV programme, you'd know that."

"Your programme *was* my favourite," I said.

"*Was? Was?* Well, goody for you. But it *wasn't* enough people's favourite. Cancelled. Gone." He threw his hands in the air and spun around in a circle. "That's why I'm here, rescuing this stupid town. No more TV for Rex Rangler."

"That's no excuse for kidnapping my grandma."

He snapped the light beam in my face. "You aren't listening. *Your grandma is gone! Forever!* Ghosts are like an echo ringing through the canyons. Nobody believes an echo is really a person talking. Ghosts are not people either."

That's exactly what I'd thought before I met Adams and saw Grandma. I'd only wanted to find ghosts so I could become famous. Vicki believed, but I didn't. But now that I had seen Grandma, I knew ghosts were people. She was my grandma, not an echo in a canyon. And I loved her.

"That's a lie. I talked to my grandma. She is a person. She's the same as she always was, just a bit harder to touch. And she wants out."

"Nonsense," Rangler said. "And that's not going to happen. Those ghosts, or should we call them echo-plasm? Hey, that's clever. *Echo-plasm.* Get it? I combined echo with ectoplasm. Pretty funny, eh?"

"Pretty pathetic."

"No, it is funny. Ha, ha. Anyway, those echo-plasms are worth millions of pounds to me," Rangler said. "When people discover that I can control real ghosts, they'll come from everywhere to see, and pay to do it. I won't need TV to be famous. And this town will get back on its feet again and people will work. Maybe even your dad will find another job. Who knows? It's possible. Don't you want that? Don't you want to see people happy and working again? Or are the echoes of the dead more important to you than the living?"

I did want my dad to get another job, especially as I'd just lost him his new one. But the ghosts didn't belong to him.

And not all the people in that black hole were ghosts.

"My friend is in there too. And she's still alive. I'm pretty sure that kidnapping girls is illegal."

Rangler froze like an icy lolly at the South Pole. "There's that ugly word again. What kidnapping? What girl?"

"Vicki."

"What's a Vicki?"

"She's my friend – the one who asks all the questions," I said.

"Funny, she looked more like a Jessica to me. Oh, well. So?"

"So Brick sucked her up inside that thing of yours," I said, pointing to the ball. "He put her in there with the ghosts, but she's not a ghost."

"That's a lie, my friend," he said. "Clever, but still a lie. What you're describing is impossible." He turned and walked over to a laptop computer sitting on a table near the ball. "We make videos of every ghost echo we capture, so I'll prove that there's no 'Vicki' inside there."

I watched as the light from the screen danced across Rangler's face. Suddenly he looked around in a panic, his eyes glazing over, searching for something he couldn't see. "You're lying. There's no girl in there. There can't be. You're just trying to make me let the ghosts out. Well, it's not going to work."

"You saw her, didn't you?" I said. "Vicki's inside that thing, and you better let her out."

"No! No! Impossible! Where are those lights?" Rangler tugged at his hair. "Why doesn't anyone listen?!"

He looked away and stared at the floor, whispering to himself. "It's not true. It's not true. Everything is going according to plan. You did everything right. Nothing is wrong."

In another second Rangler turned back to me. "Go away, you're bothering me."

"Not without Vicki, and my grandma."

BANG!

We both jumped at the sound of crashing from the dino hall. Things were falling like dominoes, one after the other. The whole place roared like it was collapsing, dino robots and skeletons smashing to the ground. Then a scream like a wounded donkey echoed through the room. They had Luke too.

A second later the emergency back-up lights snapped on. In the dim light I could see prop fronts of rickety old buildings from old towns that had been torn down. Next to them were decaying graveyards surrounded by iron fences. Stuffed black cats stared down at me from gnarled trees, and fake bats bounced up and down overhead. And in the middle of the room was a black spot, an immense hole to another world. The size of a hot-air balloon, it hovered five metres off the floor, steaming and hissing. The permanent containment unit.

"Welcome to Ghostville." Rangler swept his arms out in a spin. He acted like he'd never seen me before. "You're the very first visitor. How do you like it?"

"I want my grandma, and Vicki."

"Stubbornness is sometimes a good characteristic." Rangler dashed back to his laptop. "But not in your case." He punched the keyboard. "Give me a second, and I'll grant your wish."

Beep, beep.

My pocket buzzed. I pulled out my ecto-meter and looked at the green letters scrolling by.

Dan, it's Grandma. Please help. Something's happening.

Green steam erupted in gigantic bursts, fogging over the whole exhibit hall. Rangler typed in more commands.

Beep, beep. Another message scrawled across the screen. *Dan, it's me, Vicki. Why didn't you tell me it was so weird in here?*

I did, I wrote back. *Are you okay? What's going on?*

Vicki typed, *The ghosts are starting to fade, and these stairs that go nowhere are moving; they're collapsing on us. I've got an idea. Why don't you—*

I didn't have time to read, but, I was pretty sure what she was going to say. Sprinting across the room, I raced to get to the computer before Rangler finished. I reached out to knock the computer away, but he threw out a hand and pushed me to the floor as if I was nothing. I slid away in a big heap.

Sometimes being only a boy is frustrating.

Rangler punched the last key, roaring with laughter. The ball's outer surface peeled away like smoke in the wind and a stream of wispy forms took shape in the mist. They separated from the black hole and hovered around the room. The pink woman with her yappy poodle twirled and spun around me. Adams stalked by with his musket while Mr Greensocks took tickets.

And there was Grandma.

"Grandma! It's me!"

She didn't hear or see me. Her face was blank,

her eyes unblinking. She went past me as if I wasn't there.

"Do you like it?" Rangler laughed. "Isn't it wonderful? So real, so lifelike. Well not lifelike, but afterlifelike. Get it? *Afterlife*like? Ha! I need to write all these great catchphrases down. Pure gold. Anyway, it's a miracle, and it's going to make me famous, *more* famous. I'll never be cancelled again." He reeled and danced right along with the ghosts.

Beep beep. The ecto-meter chirped again.

Help Dan! I feel funny, like I'm fading too. I think I might—

The screen went blank.

Fading? That didn't sound good.

A few seconds later I spotted a short girl with long brown hair emerge from the cloud around the ball, chewing on a huge wad of gum.

It was Vicki.

CHAPTER TWENTY

GRAND OPENING

I stood in the middle of Ghostville, watching the giant containment unit buzz and Rex Rangler cackle with glee. The hall filled with ghosts. Misty, transparent shapes flew everywhere. Rangler must have captured every ghost in the county.

Ghosts wandered through the creaking old houses, popping out from behind doors and flying through windows. They laughed and screamed in my face. My skin crawled, but not because I was scared of the ghosts. I was scared *for* them. They should be free to live their afterlives the way they wanted, not as puppets in an amusement park.

"Vicki?" I looked up and down for her. "Vicki! Answer me!" I crossed my fingers, hoping she wasn't one of the puppets.

A ghost floated by my head, blew a bubble and drifted away to stir a smoking cauldron.

"Vicki!"

She didn't answer or even look, just kept on stirring the pot.

I noticed Rangler poke the screen. The ghosts moved to a new spot and let out howling noises. He *was* pulling their strings.

"Stop it! They're people!"

Rangler laughed and flicked the screen again. Grandma scooped up the ghost of a cat and flew over my head, cackling like a witch. She'd never have dreamed of doing that when she was alive. I was pretty sure she didn't know how to fly, plus she was allergic to cats.

I had to do something. This haunted show could go on forever. People would line up for tickets and walk through the exhibit, pointing and gawking at Grandma for years and she'd never be free. My class would come, just like we did to the opening of the Dino Barn. I could hear them laughing and screaming and making fun of the ghosts. Mr Brakenbush might wonder what happened to Vicki and how weird it was that a ghost looked just like her, even raising her hand all the time. But he'd never guess it was really her. And if I told the police or anyone, who would believe me?

The containment unit hovered like a dark sun. Lightning bolts shot up from the floor, bright beams of energy holding it in the air. It must have got its power from somewhere other than the lights. Dad's attack on the transformer hadn't shut it down. But if I could cut off that stream the whole thing might stop working.

The closer I moved to the beams of electricity, the more my skin prickled. My hair stood up straight, my ears buzzed and I started to shake. It was like that time – okay, *times* – that Luke dared me to wee on the electric fence around the horse pasture we passed on our way home from school.

Stepping back from the waves of electricity, I looked around for something better than my face to disrupt the flow. I felt a lump in my pocket — dino poo, the real stuff. I still had a couple of rocks, so I whipped one out and hurled it into the stream. As the fossil poo hit the electric bolts, a fizzling blue crackle leaped through the air, hitting me right between the eyes.

"OUCH!"

I wanted to touch my nose, but I was afraid it wasn't there, just a smoking hole with my brains peeking out.

That hurt! Much worse than weeing on an electric fence!

"Careful." Rangler wagged his finger. "No touching."

My head twirled as fast as the spirits that spun around the room. Everything I'd tried had blown up in my face. The way Rangler laughed I was pretty sure I'd end up another ghost like Vicki.

Vicki.

As fast as I could I texted,

How do I cut back-up power?

I stared at the screen but there was no answer. Maybe Vicki wasn't in there anymore. Maybe she really had become a ghost and was floating around the room with the others. A cold stone dropped into my stomach.

The room shook like an earthquake that rattled the floor so hard I almost fell over again. Rangler stopped laughing and turned towards the entrance. His jaw dropped and he grabbed the computer and ducked behind the streams of electricity.

We weren't alone.

Charging through the door and stomping on the turnstiles was a giant tyrannosaurus robot. It smashed into the hall, huge metal mouth hanging open showing 30-centimetre-long teeth. I gaped at it, my heart racing. I thought dinosaurs were cool, but this one looked as if it wanted to eat me.

The dinosaurs were haunted too!

Rumbling like a freight train, the robot took three gigantic steps towards me. I dived out of the way, but the monster followed me towards the far side of the room. Just as I backed into a corner it stopped and the head dropped to the ground, resting its jaw on the floor. Its teeth dripped robot spit. I'd come all this way to rescue ghosts, and now I was going to be eaten by a haunted robot dinosaur.

I gazed at the teeth while I inched further into the corner, my back pressed hard against the wall. There was no more room. I imagined those razor-sharp fangs cutting through me. I opened my mouth to scream when I spotted something behind the teeth.

"Look, Dan. I'm driving a dinosaur!"

"Luke?" I let out my breath and felt really glad I hadn't screamed in front of him.

He grinned and waved. "I jumped in when those

guards chased me. This thing's got controls like a video game. They ran away like chickens. Want to try it? It's amazing."

I had a better idea. "Is there room for me in there, too?"

"No," Luke said. "It's only got one pilot's seat."

I pointed at the containment unit. "Okay. See if you can stop that electricity."

Luke's eyes popped. "I thought you said it was a small black ball – that thing's huge."

I shrugged. "I wouldn't need a dinosaur for a small one."

"That's lightning, Dan. I could get electrocuted. I remember that electric fence."

I shook my head. "Don't wee on it! Just stick the dino in far enough to cut off the flow."

Luke shook his head. "I don't know. Lightning."

Maybe he was right. I touched my smoking nose. It was still there, but it hurt like crazy. "I've got another idea. Can you pick up anything in that mouth?"

Now Luke's eyes lit up. "I think so. I just have to make sure I don't bite too hard."

I pointed at Rangler, still typing commands into the computer. I didn't care how hard Luke bit. "Get him!"

Luke let out a whoop and fired up the robot. It staggered to its feet and turned around. The tail swooshed right over my head, parting my hair. Luke lifted one leg, crashed it down, and then another, stomping right at Rangler. The old TV host cowered behind the protection of the electric arcs. It didn't take Luke long to forget about getting electrocuted.

"Luke! Watch out!"

The tyrannosaurus lit up in a spray of blue, green, yellow and red sparks like a firework display. Electricity streamed over and around its body until it glowed like a rainbow. The legs wobbled and the giant machine leaned over just out of range of the electric arc, ready to fall.

"Luke!" I screamed, racing over to him. "Luke? Are you okay?"

"Dan," he whispered, his voice sounding groggy. "Want to get a drink? Buuurrrrpppp!" Then he leaned back, burped again and rolled up into a ball. I thought I could hear him snoring.

I reached up and pulled on the little door under

the T. rex's neck. "Let me in," I said. I tugged on the handle. No luck. The door was stuck fast. "Luke! Open the door!"

"Later, I'm sleeping."

Luke was out of it. I needed another answer.

A giant crackle sounded behind me. Vicki's ghost, or whatever it was, hovered nearby, looking at the prison globe. The containment unit sizzled and sparked. Then a small spot appeared on the underside. White against the black, it grew bigger and bigger, pushing out like the bump I got on my head when Luke tested his home-built catapult while I was standing in front of it.

Splurp!

A blob, covered in greyish, dripping, jelly-like goo, dropped out onto the floor and rolled out of reach of the electrostatic charges. Then it jumped up into a crouch and raised two hands, fingers extended like talons, up over its head like a ninja.

"EEEEEEYYYYYYAAAAAA!" It screamed and ran straight at Rangler.

Rex glanced over his shoulder at the shout but was too slow to see the goo-blob coming. It took a flying-dragon leap, stuck out its right foot and kicked Rangler square in the bum like a kangaroo on steroids.

"Hey!" He shrieked and fell forward, his moustache waving from an impact stronger than a Luke-powered burp. Stumbling towards the robot, Rangler clanked his head against the dino's left knee and stood there, arching his eyebrows. "Ouch! That hurt!" he cried, rubbing his head.

Then the dino's leg started to creak. First it wiggled. Then it wobbled. Then it waggled. Then it twisted and twined like a rubber band. Finally it buckled. The robot monster tilted and whipped around towards Rangler. I jumped back and the goo-ninja ran the other way. Rangler stood like he was glued in place. The T. rex's mouth gaped open, razor-sharp teeth flashing, and with a roaring crash it smacked down on the hard concrete floor right on top of the ghostnapper. Rows of teeth like prison bars knifed into the floor spreading tiny cracks like spiderwebs around my feet. The teeth surrounded Rangler. He was trapped, eaten by his own fake dinosaur.

A second later the dino's belly popped open. Luke must have got the door unstuck, because he slipped out of the hatch, his hair standing up and his hands shaking. I guessed his nap was over.

"I think I fried my brains."

"We did it!" I jumped up and down and slapped Luke on the shoulder.

"Ouch!" He grinned and slapped me back, so I punched him.

He got ready to swing at me when I grabbed his hand. "Come on," I said. "We've got one more thing to do."

I turned around, looking for the goo-thing that had knocked Rangler into his prison. I needed to ask it if Vicki was okay. It was scraping slime from its face.

"Hi, Dan!"

"Vicki!" I cried. "It's you! You're okay!"

"Of course," she said. "Who else do you know who got sucked into a ghost vacuum so you could escape and work out how to defeat Rangler?" She grinned and wiped more of the sticky gunk away. It covered her entire body with a centimetre of goo and looked much worse than the fake dino poo she'd screamed over, but she wasn't acting disgusted now. I must have been getting to her.

"I was scared when you didn't answer my message," I said. "How did you get out?"

"Easy. Everyone else in there was a ghost and couldn't touch anything. Then I remembered how I pulled you out before, so I just decided to push, and boom! I'm here. It was pretty gross, though," she added, wiping a handful of goo on me.

"Yuck!" I said. She was learning.

Vicki giggled. "Why's your nose all red?"

"I tried to stick my face in a bolt of lightning."

"Why are you always shoving your head into things?" She reached up and smeared some gunk on my nose. "I think this acts like an insulator. That's why I didn't get electrocuted."

"Hey, that feels good," I said, rubbing the cool slime into my nose. "Thanks."

Just then her ghost zoomed by and floated right in between us. Vicki stopped and her mouth gaped open. "Is that me?" she asked. "I don't chew my gum that way. That's gross." She waved her hand at her apparition. "Go away. Get lost!" Then she kicked at it. The gum-smacking ghost flew up to the ceiling.

"I don't get it," I said. "How can both of you be here at the same time? Aren't those the real ghosts?"

Vicki shook her head. "I don't think so. The ghosts are still trapped. Those are just projections. And not very good ones. My hair does not look like that."

I decided not to tell her that it did.

"Yes it does," Luke said. "But worse."

Vicki slapped him with a handful of gunk.

"But you said you were fading," I said.

"It felt like that," Vicki said. "I think some sort of projector scanned me and I started to turn invisible. But then I came back. That's when I worked out how to climb out."

"Wait," I said. "If the ghosts aren't out yet, then we still have work to do."

Vicki nodded. "You're right. Let's go!" she said, snapping back into her ninja pose.

Rangler had dropped the laptop when he fell. Vicki and I raced over and she said, "I think you should hit control—"

No time. I jumped up and down on it, smashing the machine into tiny pieces. I'd always wanted to do that.

"Now we're done," I said.

Nothing happened.

I looked over at the giant floating black hole and stopped cold. The containment ball still hummed and the ghosts still danced.

Rangler laughed from behind his tooth prison. "Problem?"

I shivered. "I broke the computer," I said to Vicki. "Why aren't the ghosts free?"

"Um," Vicki said. "I was going to say that if you hit control-F10-delete, I think that's how you deactivate it."

"How did you work that out?"

"A ghost told me," she said.

"Okay." I leaned over and punched the keys. Little plastic lettered squares fell out on the floor, cracked and broken. "Oops!"

"Now what do we do?" Vicki asked.

There was only one thing left. I leaned into the teeth and grabbed Rangler's coat. "How do we shut the containment unit down and let the ghosts free?"

When I grabbed him, Rangler's moustache slipped off his lip and dangled around his neck. It was fake too.

The only things that were real were the ghosts, and possibly his eyebrows.

"Sorry to disappoint you," he said, brushing my hands away and straightening his jacket. "But I'll just wait for the police to come and arrest you. I'm sure they'll take my side. I'm a big man in this town. I'm famous."

I looked at Vicki and Luke. "We have to turn that thing off."

Luke shook his head and threw up his hands. "The dinosaur didn't work. And I totally smashed up that egress sign."

Rangler laughed again and his suit flashed in a rainbow of colours. "I'm the only one who knows how to turn it off, and I'm not telling."

This man was seriously crazy. I had no more ideas, and another dinosaur wasn't going to come crashing through the door.

Just then my ecto-meter beeped. The screen read: *suit*.

"Suit? What does that mean?"

Rangler snorted. "You'll never get it. Probably means *lawsuit*, which is coming your way. I hope your parents have money. Oh, that's right, someone's dad just lost his job." He sniggered again, turned a knob on his remote control and the rainbow switched to flashing red like a stop light.

I texted back.

I don't get it.

I stared at the screen, waiting for an answer. Nothing.

"What's the answer?" I shouted at the ball.

Still no text.

I slapped at my head and looked at Luke, but he just shrugged.

The ecto-meter beeped. *Suit*, was all it said.

An idea struggled to get out of my head. I'd noticed Rangler tuck the control back in his pocket. Is that what the message meant, his clothes? I only had one choice. I shoved my head in again. Then I reached through the tyrannosaurus's teeth and pulled the controls for Rangler's Christmas tree suit out of his pocket.

"No!!!! Give that back!"

Jackpot!

I put my thumb on the switch.

Rangler screamed, wild-eyed. "Don't! It's booby-trapped. You'll blow up the whole town!"

I looked at Vicki. "He's lying," she said, shaking her head. "I hope."

She didn't sound too certain.

"No way," Luke said. "But that would be cool."

I squeezed the control box.

"Listen, Dan," Rangler said, holding his hands together and pleading. "I'll give your dad his job back. Even let your grandmother go. Just don't push that button. You'll ruin me. You don't want that. Remember all the fun times you had watching my programmes? I was your favourite."

I looked at Vicki and grinned. "You *were* my favourite." Then I flipped the OFF switch. Suddenly the sizzling electricity under the ball exploded, shooting up to the ceiling in huge zigzags of lightning. The whole building rocked with thunder.

Vicki, Luke and I ran for cover.

I had blown up the whole town!

Then the crackling stopped, and the lightning bolts

shrank back into the floor. The containment unit still hung in the air, but after a few seconds it started to shimmer and flash just like Rangler's clothes. In a rush the ghosts stopped screeching and swooping and winked out.

"Where'd they go?" Luke asked. "You killed them."

Uh-oh.

"No, look." Vicki pointed at the ghost ball.

The outside of the giant sphere slowly peeled away as wispy layers wafted into a thin mist. Then with a great *SPLAT,* like a Luke-tossed water balloon hitting me in the face, a downpour of goo splashed onto the floor. Fog steamed up from the giant puddle. From the cloud, one by one, shadowy figures emerged and floated out to encircle us, laughing and hugging each other. The ghostly howls were replaced by the roar of cheering and hands clapping.

"We're free! We're free! You did it! We're free!"

Grandma glided up and wrapped her arms around me, although she still couldn't touch me. "Oh, Dan. I knew I could count on you. You're such a smart, grown-up, brave boy."

I tried to hug her back, but ended up hugging myself.

"Thanks, Grandma. I'm glad you're okay."

She smiled big and wide, beaming at me. I could feel her glow all through my body. We were going to be together again.

I felt warm all over. "Vicki, did you meet my Grand—?" I looked around for Vicki. She wasn't there.

Grandma hovered beside me. "Don't worry, dear, she'll be here in a second. She's a bit busy at the moment."

I glanced around the room, finally spotting Vicki by the old cinema set. A man in an Army uniform knelt on one knee in front of her. She nodded and waving her arms threw a kick. She must have been telling her story.

"You have a very nice girlfriend," Grandma said.

Luke sniggered. "See, g-i-r-l-f-ahhh, whatever. I told you."

"Shut up!"

I looked at Grandma. "Who is that she's talking to? Is that her— "

She nodded. "Yes."

In another minute Vicki and the ghost soldier walked over to Grandma and me.

"Dan," Vicki said, beaming. "This is the man who worked out how to turn off the controls and taught me that flying kick. Meet my dad."

CHAPTER TWENTY-ONE

MOVING ON

Vicki and I sat on the floor in the middle of Ghostville with my Grandma and her dad. The ghosts were all free now, and Rangler was down for the count.

"This is so great that we can all be here," Vicki said, smiling wider than I'd ever seen. Her face was easier to see now that she'd washed most of the goo off. "I always wanted you to meet my dad."

Her dad, whose name was Jacob Winters, Scrgeant Jacob Winters, knew all about electronics and had worked out Rangler's secret controls. "I'm glad to see Vicki is making new friends," he said. "You both should be proud of yourselves."

Vicki touched my hand. "Well done. I knew I could count on you."

"You too," I told her.

She looked over at Rangler, trapped in his dino prison. He sat on the floor, twirling his moustache. "You got him." She smiled.

"*We* got him."

My heart beat like a hummingbird's wings, what with her dad right there, but I grabbed Vicki's hand and helped her up. Luke giggled.

"Shut up!"

"Told you," he said.

Vicki looked down at her hand in mine and then over at her dad, who smiled at her. "I always feel safe when my dad holds my hand. He's the best." Then in a whisper so her dad couldn't hear, "He likes you. He thinks you're really brave."

Luke heard. He gagged on his finger.

Vicki slapped his shoulder. "Grow up!"

★ ★ ★

Well, now that I'd found real ghosts, set them free, become friends with the weird girl, lost my dad his job and defeated evil for all time, I sat down to talk to Grandma. I had my plans all ready for her to move in with us. She could have my bedroom and I'd have the one downstairs. Then I wouldn't have to listen to my dad snoring and Luke and I, and Vicki too, could play video games without being nagged. And as Grandma was a ghost she didn't need to eat. Maybe she could even help Dad get another job by scaring somebody into hiring him. It was a perfect plan without any holes.

"What do you think, Grandma? I haven't told Mum or Dad yet, but Dad is outside and knows all about you and the other ghosts. I'm sure it won't be a problem. He even helped me by shutting down the power." I nodded in agreement for her. "It'll be great. Maybe you could even help me find other ghosts and get on TV. I know you probably don't want to be famous, but maybe someone else does."

Grandma smiled and stroked my hair, or pretended to. "You mean like you?"

"I'm pretty much over that." I glanced at Rangler, stuck in his dino-tooth cell. "Famous isn't so great."

"Oh, Dan, you're such a sweet, sweet boy," she said. "I love you so much. Nothing would make me happier than to come and live with you and have you sit on my lap again while I read you stories."

I knew I was too big for her lap, but the rest sounded good.

"I'll tell Dad," I said, jumping up.

Grandma grabbed at my hand. "But . . ."

I stopped and looked back at her. "But what?"

"But I'm afraid it doesn't work that way."

"What do you mean? What doesn't work that way?"

Grandma smiled and looked around, motioning towards the other ghosts. I hadn't noticed before, but they were all gathered together in a group at the far end of the hall. A few stopped to shake their fists at Rangler, who was still trapped inside the tyrannosaurus's mouth, but then they quickly joined the others. One by one all the ghosts started to shimmer and flicker, like a light bulb about to burn out. In a few seconds they were gone.

"What's happening? Are they going back to haunt their old houses? I think most of them were torn down. We might have to find other places for them to haunt. Maybe the old museum?"

"No, dear." Grandma's voice was soft, sounding like when she'd first told me that she was ill. "It's time for them to go. They're moving on. Most ghosts only stay a while, but we were trapped here by that awful man until you rescued us. Our time here is over. My time is over."

I choked on my breath and the room shrank in around me. "No. You can't go, not now that I've set you free."

"But you did set me free," Grandma said. "It's time for me to use that freedom."

"What about Vicki's dad?" I turned towards Vicki. She and her dad were back by the old cinema that she'd told me they'd always gone to. She wasn't practising kicks anymore. This time she was wiping her eyes.

"We all have to go." Grandma smiled big and bright and a glow emerged from behind her eyes, streaming out to touch me with its warmth. The shine quickly spread to her whole body and she turned so bright I had to squint to see her. In another second she drifted towards the ceiling and flickered like the others.

"Bye, Dan," Grandma said with a little wave of her hand. "I love you. You'll always be my hero."

I watched her float off and slowly fade away. This time I was there to see her leave.

"Bye, Grandma." I didn't care if Luke saw me cry. "I love you, too."

And then she was gone. Forever.

I sniffed and wiped my eyes. Vicki walked over. She hung her head and looked down at her feet, her face hidden behind her fringe. She held out her hand and I took it.

Her dad had faded away, too. All the ghosts had left. All except one.

* * *

Vicki, Luke and I stood in the hallway after school, waiting for all the other children to clear out. Vicki double checked for teachers and then popped a wad of gum into her mouth. She chomped excitedly as I prepared to get a failed bubble spit at me. I'd tried to show Vicki how to blow bubbles, but I'm not any good either and we both got tired of picking gum out of each other's hair.

"Okay." She scanned her checklist. "Tomorrow's Saturday so we have to get up early to go to the cemetery to mow and weed around Adams's statue."

Luke groaned.

"I already have to mow my own lawn," I said. "My dad's teaching me to cut straight lines."

"Dan." Vicki put her hands on her hips. "You

promised. We told Adams that in exchange for helping us find lost ghosts, who we could help move on, we'd keep his grave clean. Besides, I asked your dad and he said you could wait until Sunday to mow the lawn."

That's what I get for inviting Vicki over for pizza. She conspires with Dad.

"And look." She waved a sheet of paper at me. "I've got the petition to make the second Saturday in August Richard Adams Pioneer's Day, with a parade, fireworks, ice cream and everything. After we mow and scrub the statue, we have to go out and get signatures."

Signatures?! Mowing?! Scrubbing?! How come nobody told me being friends with a girl was so much work? Well, nobody but Luke, but who listens to him?

"But that statue is covered with bird poo. It's yucky."

Vicki shook her head. "You promised."

Suddenly I got goosebumps and the feeling I was being watched. Vicki smiled at something behind me, and even though they'd stopped hating each other I knew it couldn't be Luke.

"Much obliged to you for keeping the old statue pigeon free." Adams floated near the ceiling in his battered old jacket and hat. He'd decided not to move on until he'd helped all the other lost ghosts in town, to make up for letting his friends get kidnapped by Rangler. "I'm popular with the birdies," he said, "so the poo has built up over time. It may take a bit of elbow grease – and a strong stomach."

"Ugh!"

Suddenly lawn mowing seemed like fun.

"Pssst." Vicki held back a giggle and put her hand to her mouth so Luke couldn't hear her. "That's what Luke's for."

Luke did have the strongest stomach I'd ever seen, and nobody is more amazed by old poo.

I winked at her and pulled out my ecto-meter. Down to business. I pointed it at the door in front of us. *GIRLS*. I crossed my fingers and hoped Jessica wasn't in there again. The ecto-meter beeped a couple of times and the little green line on the screen danced up and down.

"Contact. Someone's definitely at home."

"Everybody ready?" Vicki asked.

I nodded and Adams tipped his hat.

"Ready for what?" Luke said.

"Good. Let's do it. EEEEEEYYYYYAAAA!!!" Vicki screeched, jumped into her ninja stance, arms raised, hands looking like hawk talons, picked up her foot with a high-flying karate kick and planted it right in the middle of the door. It whipped open and we rushed inside. Screams and flying hair filled the air.

Well, at least no one can blame this one on me.

They can't say Vicki isn't supposed to be in the girls' toilets.

ABOUT THE AUTHOR

John Bladek grew up in Washington, USA. When he was young, he liked to listen to ghost stories on the radio and sneak into the basement on Friday nights to watch a scary TV programme his mum didn't approve of. He no longer hides under his pillow after visiting the haunted house down the road, but he still remembers those scary tales. Since then John earned a PhD in History, where all ghosts come from, loves to play trivia, and wonders why they don't make hauntable houses anymore.

ABOUT THE COVER ILLUSTRATOR

Born in the UK in 1988, **Charlie Bowater** was raised on '90s cartoons and as much Disney as she could get her hands on. Growing up, she insisted that one day she would be an animator. Although that changed a bit, her love of art never has!

She lives in the north east of England, and works as a Senior Concept Artist. The rest of the time she's an illustrator and doodler of anything and everything else.

GLOSSARY

abyss a dark, empty place where nothing exists

awning a cover made of canvas or other material that shades or shelters like a roof

covert secret

egress way out or exit

injustice unjust act or a violation of another's rights

nemesis formidable and usually victorious rival or opponent

paranormal having to do with an unexplained event that has no scientific explanation

phenomenon something very unusual or remarkable

prehistoric living or occurring before people began to record history

pursuit act of trying to obtain something

spectre ghost